"You hurt me, Dylan. Because what you think you want and what you really want are two different things."

"I want you," he whispered, backing her up against the wall. "*You* are what I think I want and what I really want."

"But you might change your mind." Shelby began to look away again.

"I am not going to change my mind." Dylan brought his hands up on either side of her head, burrowing his fingers in her damp hair. "I hurt you, because I'm so used to pushing everyone away, and I'm sorry. You are what I want. I won't hurt you again."

Dylan could see the doubt in Shelby's eyes, and it killed him. He was afraid she would pull away. But she leaned toward him, putting her lips gently against his.

He kissed her back gently. But then the hunger—the *heat*—that had sparked between them since the first moment they'd met flared again. And all thought of soft and gentle was left behind.

LEVERAGE

—

Janie Crouch

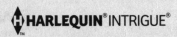

To my "Shelby": soul mates come in all different forms,
in all different seasons. Thank you for the love you radiate
and helping me see the beauty in everything.
May the wine of our friendship never run dry.

ISBN-13: 978-0-373-74900-3

Leverage

Copyright © 2015 by Janie Crouch

Recycling programs
for this product may
not exist in your area.

Printed in U.S.A.

Janie Crouch has loved to read romance her whole life. She cut her teeth on Harlequin Romance novels as a preteen, then moved on to a passion for romantic suspense as an adult. Janie lives with her husband and four children overseas. Janie enjoys traveling, long-distance running, movie-watching, knitting and adventure/obstacle racing. You can find out more about her at janiecrouch.com.

Books by Janie Crouch

Omega Sector series

Infiltration
Countermeasures
Untraceable
Leverage

HARLEQUIN INTRIGUE

Primal Instinct

CAST OF CHARACTERS

Dylan Branson—Oldest of the Branson siblings. Charter pilot and former Omega Sector agent tasked with making sure the codes in Shelby's possession are brought to Omega as soon as possible.

Shelby Keelan—Quirky computer game programmer. She found hidden codes in a children's computer game and realized they were links to a terrorist attack.

Dennis Burgamy—Dylan's ex-boss at Omega Sector. Seems to care more about his own reputation than the safety of his agents.

Chantelle DiMuzio—Dennis Burgamy's harried assistant and vital member of the Omega Sector team.

Megan Fuller-Branson—Shelby's best friend from college and Dylan's sister-in-law. Computer genius and Omega Sector employee. Five months pregnant.

Sawyer Branson—Megan's husband and father of her unborn child. Dylan's youngest brother and Omega Sector agent.

Cameron Branson—Dylan's brother and Omega Sector agent. Married to Sophia Reardon-Branson.

Juliet Branson—Dylan's sister and Omega Sector agent. Engaged to Evan Karcz.

Sophia Reardon-Branson—Cameron's wife and graphic artist for the FBI.

Evan Karcz—The Branson brothers' best friend. Omega Sector agent. Engaged to Juliet Branson.

Chapter One

Sometimes a man just wanted to be left alone.

Dylan Branson didn't think that was too much to ask. He'd served his country for years, both on American soil and off, and had the scars—both physical and emotional—to show for it. But that was behind him now. Far behind him.

Not that you would know it from the voice talking at Dylan from the phone.

Dylan held the phone out at arm's length, staring at it as if it were a snake about to bite him. He'd rather be handling a snake. Seriously, give him a cottonmouth over what was at the other end of this phone line.

It was Dennis Burgamy, Dylan's boss when he worked at Omega Sector, a covert interagency task force. A crime-fighting, problem-solving, *get-stuff-done* unit, made up of the most elite agents the country had to offer. And Dylan had been one of the best of the best.

But not anymore.

Despite its arm's-length distance, Dylan could still hear Dennis Burgamy clearly on the other line. Dylan hadn't held the phone against his ear in at least two minutes, but evidently Burgamy hadn't missed Dylan's input into the conversation because the other man hadn't even noticed Dylan wasn't talking.

Which was pretty typical of Dylan's former boss. The difference now was that Dylan didn't have to listen to the other man. Burgamy wasn't his boss anymore.

Finally silence came from the other end of the phone. Dylan cautiously brought it back to his ear.

"Are you there, Branson?"

"Yeah, I'm here." Dylan sat on the porch of the house he'd mostly built himself and looked out over the pinkish light of early evening hitting the Blue Ridge Mountains surrounding him on three sides. Those mountains had been the only thing able to bring him a measure of peace over the past few years since his wife's death, and he tried to draw on that peace again now. To no avail. "You do remember that I don't work for you anymore, right, Burgamy?"

Dylan's statement was met with a dramatic sigh. There had never been any lost love between Burgamy and any of the Branson siblings. Dylan's sister and two brothers were all active Omega agents, and all had butted heads with Burgamy at some point.

"You are in the charter airline business now, Dylan," Burgamy reminded him. "I'm not asking you to do anything you wouldn't do for any other paying customer."

It was true. For the past four years Dylan had been flying customers and cargo wherever they needed to go all over the East Coast with his Cessna. But Dylan wasn't so desperate for business that he wanted to be at Burgamy's beck and call.

"I'm all booked. Sorry."

"Look, Dylan…" Dylan recognized the change in Burgamy's tone. Evidently Burgamy realized threatening Dylan wouldn't get him what he wanted, so he'd decided to try a different tactic. "How about if you do this for us, then I'll erase all record of Sawyer's little incident last year."

The *little incident* referred to Dylan's youngest brother, Sawyer, punching Burgamy in the jaw and knocking his boss unconscious during an operation that was going wrong. Sawyer managed to keep his job at Omega, but only barely. And although Sawyer was able to keep his job, the occurrence would still keep his brother from ever being able to move up in official ranks. Of course, until recently, Sawyer had no interest in ever moving higher than the rank of agent. Doing so would mean a desk job, which had frightened him no end. But now that Sawyer was married to sweet little Megan and expecting a baby, a desk job might be more appealing to him.

And damn it, this made saying no to Burgamy much more complicated.

Dylan looked out at the mountains. He didn't want to set foot back inside Omega. He'd done it a couple of times since he'd quit over six years ago, and each time had been fraught with disaster. Dylan still had residual discomfort from the beating he'd taken while trying to help his brother Cameron on an Omega mission a while ago.

In Dylan's experience, every trip to Omega led to some sort of pain. And he wasn't interested in experiencing that again if he had any other option.

"It's important, Branson," Burgamy continued. "We need these codes. And Shelby Keelan, the lady with the codes, is a friend of your sister-in-law. I'm sure Megan will take it as a personal insult if you don't help us with this matter."

Dylan closed his eyes. Burgamy didn't know it, but Dylan was already in. And if Dylan hadn't been, bringing up Megan would've done it. Dylan liked Sawyer's wife—the brilliant computer scientist—a great deal. She was good for his brother; had somehow managed to tame the playboy of the family without even trying.

And now Sawyer and Megan were having a

baby. Which was totally great for Dylan's parents, who had wanted grandkids for the longest time. They'd finally get their wish.

For just a second, that old ache crept into Dylan's chest. He pushed away the thought of the baby that hadn't made it when his wife had been killed. Nothing could be done about that now.

If Megan wanted him to pick up some codes or whatever from a friend of hers and bring the codes to Omega, Dylan would do it. He loved his brother, loved his sister-in-law and wanted to do anything he could to keep that baby growing happy and healthy inside her.

Of course, he didn't know why Megan's friend couldn't just email the codes. Why Dylan needed to hand deliver them to Washington, DC. Or why this lady couldn't just deliver them herself. But whatever. He knew better than to ask. With Omega, things were never simple.

Effective? Yes. Simple? No.

For example, things could've been much simpler if Megan or Sawyer had just called Dylan themselves and asked him to fly in the codes. He'd already be gassing up his Cessna right now. But Burgamy couldn't resist an opportunity to lord power over any member of the Branson family. It bugged Dylan to submit to Burgamy, but he might as well get it over with.

"Fine, Burgamy, I'll do it."

"Good. Because Shelby Keelan is on her way to you right now. She should be arriving in Falls Run in about thirty minutes. Meeting you at the only restaurant your blip on the map seems to have."

Dylan hung up the phone without saying anything else. Burgamy had obviously told the woman to come out here even before asking Dylan, sure he would get Dylan's cooperation. Dylan hated being a foregone conclusion.

He watched the pinkening sky for a few more moments, allowing the phone to fall next to him in the swing on his porch rather than crush it against the wall the way he wanted to.

There were things Dylan regretted about his deliberate walk away from Omega six years ago. But having to listen to Dennis Burgamy wasn't one of them.

Dylan would get the codes from Megan's friend, fly them to Omega, say a quick hello to his siblings and get the hell out. There would be no traversing up the sides of yachts, emergency takeoffs with people shooting at him or being beaten to within an inch of his life.

Like his last visits.

Dylan grabbed his phone and stood up. He'd have to get going if he was going to make it into town by the time Shelby Keelan arrived. His phone buzzed again in his hand. Dylan grimaced, hoping it wasn't Burgamy.

It wasn't.

"You are not my current favorite sibling, Sawyer." Dylan's words were tough, but his greeting held no malice.

"Ha. Well, I'm still Mom's favorite, so that's all that matters," Sawyer responded. "I guess I'm too late to catch you before Burgamy does."

"Just got off the phone with him."

"Damn it. I'm sorry, Dylan. I told Burgamy I would handle it, but you know him."

Dylan rolled his eyes. Yes, he was quite familiar with Burgamy's tactics. "Looks like I'll be delivering some codes to you tonight." Dylan looked out the window; menacing clouds were rolling in behind the setting sun. "Actually, it might be much later tonight. It looks like a storm is rolling in."

"Thanks for doing this, man. The codes are—" Sawyer broke off midsentence and Dylan could hear his muffled words to someone else before they stopped entirely.

"Dylan?" A much softer female voice came on the line.

"Hey, Megan. How are you feeling?"

"Fine now that I'm not hurling my guts out multiple times a day." Dylan could hear the smile in his petite sister-in-law's voice. "I'm sorry about Burgamy, Dylan. Sawyer wanted us to leave him out of it totally, but I wouldn't let him."

"It's no problem, hon. I can handle Burgamy."

"Thanks for meeting Shelby. She and I knew each other in college. She's…special."

Dylan didn't know what to make of *special*. That could mean a lot of things. "Well, I hope you don't mean special as in special needs like your husband."

Megan laughed. "No, Shelby is definitely not special needs. The opposite, in fact. A brilliant computer-game programmer."

"Well, either way it's no problem. I'll see you guys soon. I've got to get going if I'm going to meet Shelby on time. Burgamy didn't leave much wiggle room."

"Thanks again, Dylan."

"Anything for you, sweetheart. You just keep my little niece or nephew safe, okay? Bye."

Dylan disconnected and went inside his house of the past four years. He had never brought a woman here; he'd preferred encounters to happen at their place instead. It made leaving much easier and awkward talks about why he couldn't stay much less necessary.

Dylan preferred his solitude and planned to keep it that way. He'd tried dating, but many women thought being a widower meant he needed to be smothered with attention. With love. They wanted to wrap their arms around him and help chase his demons away. Dylan knew they meant well, but he couldn't tolerate that kind of unrelenting attention.

Dylan would face his own demons. Always had.

So he kept things casual with women, and kept them out of his personal space. Sometimes, much more rarely now, he got physically involved, but he was sure to let a woman know up front that his heart was off the table. A future with Dylan was not an option.

Dylan walked into his bedroom and changed out of the dirty work clothes he'd had on for normal plane maintenance. He decided to take a quick shower, cursing Burgamy again when he couldn't linger under the hot water to help loosen some of the residual soreness from old wounds. Thirty minutes wasn't a long time to get to Falls Run from his house.

And yes, Sally's was the only sit-down restaurant in the small town, more of a diner than anything else. There were also a couple of fast-food places, a gas station, a bar, hardware store and bank. Falls Run wasn't *that* small. And it was perfect for Dylan's purposes in a town: small enough that he didn't have to worry about too many strangers wandering around, and large enough that he was able to get what he needed regularly enough for both his business and personal needs.

He'd chosen Falls Run on purpose. At the borders of Virginia, Tennessee and North Carolina, it allowed him access, via his Cessna, to almost anywhere on the East and Gulf coasts. Plus, the town was surrounded by the Blue Ridge Mountains. In Dylan's opinion, you couldn't ask for better real estate than that.

And it was far enough from Washington, DC, and Omega for him to stay away from his past there.

Dylan rolled his eyes. At least he *thought* Falls Run was far enough away. Evidently not, given the past few years. Dylan got dressed in jeans and a button-down shirt, grabbed his keys and wallet from the dresser and headed out the door to his pickup truck.

What the hell. He'd enjoy a nice meal at Sally's—he was tired of his own cooking anyway—and meet Megan's friend. Dylan pretty much kept to himself, but he knew how to be polite and charming when he wanted to be. His mother had instilled that much in the Branson siblings when they were growing up. Shelby Keelan wasn't at fault for Burgamy's high-handed tactics; no need to blame her. He'd meet her and move on.

Get the codes. Deliver the codes. Get out.

No problem.

Chapter Two

For the first time she could remember, Shelby Keelan cursed her gifts when it came to math. Normally she was very appreciative of them: they allowed her to make a great living doing something she enjoyed—making games kids loved to play. But not this time. This time her abilities had brought her out of her nice comfortable home to a strange town to meet a strange person she had no real desire to meet.

Of course, Shelby rarely had the desire to meet anyone new.

She easily found a parking spot at the restaurant in Falls Run, although the lot was across the street from the diner due to the narrow shape of the town forced by mountains. Shelby had been told there was only one restaurant and she couldn't miss it, but she'd still been a little worried. What kind of town had only one restaurant?

Evidently the town of Falls Run.

Shelby didn't mind small towns. She didn't

mind big cities either. It was the people in both that tended to cause her stress. Shelby just didn't do people very well.

Even now, pulling into a mostly empty parking lot, she was pretty stressed out. Shelby knew she would need to make small talk. With strangers. Multiple strangers maybe. She had many talents, but chatting with people wasn't one of them. She was an introvert through and through.

Her introversion had driven her flamboyant mother crazy when Shelby was a child. Her mom wanted to show her off—as if people really wanted to hear some four-year-old recite pi to the two-hundredth digit—but young Shelby had just wanted to be alone.

Adult Shelby just wanted to be alone, too. Back at her own house in Knoxville, where everything had its place and was comfortable and safe and familiar. Where she didn't have to think too hard about what she did or what she said or if she was coming off as rude or unfriendly or standoffish.

It wasn't that Shelby was afraid of people, she really wasn't. She wasn't agoraphobic, as her mother tried so often to suggest. Wasn't afraid something terrible would happen to her if she left her house. People just…*exhausted* Shelby. So she chose to be around them as little as possible. Fortunately, she had a job developing games and software that allowed her to spend most of her time away from people. Perfect.

Plus, she had plenty of friends in her life, just mostly of the four-legged and furry variety. And none of them were disappointed when Shelby wasn't up to making small talk. They kept one another company just fine. And Shelby had a couple of the two-legged-friend versions, too.

But it took pretty grave circumstances to get Shelby to willingly leave her house and be around people she didn't know for extended periods of time as she was doing now.

Like a terrorist-attack countdown in the coding of a children's computer game. One that Shelby happened to discover two days ago. One that anyone else in the world would've missed.

But Shelby hadn't missed it, the way she never missed anything having to do with numbers. She had known immediately the numbers she saw were not part of the game. They clearly had been planted, and once Shelby dug into them a bit, she realized they were, in part, a countdown. But she couldn't figure out any more than that on her own.

Sure that she had stumbled on to something potentially criminal at best, downright sinister at worst, Shelby had emailed her computer engineering friend from their college days at MIT, Dr. Megan Fuller.

Except Megan was Dr. Megan Fuller-*Branson*

now, and expecting a little baby Dr. Fuller-Branson in a couple of months.

Shelby had explained the coding she'd found and what she suspected. Most others would've scoffed or accused Shelby of overdramatizing, but Megan and Shelby had developed a healthy respect for each other years ago at MIT. They may not be the type to chat with each other over coffee, but they took each other seriously.

And it ended up that Megan was now working with her new husband at some sort of clandestine law enforcement agency that specialized in saving-the-world type of stuff. Quite convenient for the matter at hand. Especially since the codes had been planted by some terrorist group known as DS-13, who was evidently really bad news.

Spotting the codes and realizing their nefarious purpose had been the easy part for Shelby. The hard part had come when Megan had asked Shelby to travel to Washington, DC.

Shelby understood why Megan needed her to come in. The string of coding Shelby saw in the game had only come up for a moment before deleting itself. Very few people would've been looking at the game in its raw-data form, and nobody would've been able to catch the countdown codes and the coordinates embedded in it in the split second it was available.

Unless you were Shelby, who was able to memorize thousands of numbers at once just by looking at them. A complete photographic memory when it came to numbers. And coding, whether it be as innocent as games, or as deadly as a potential terrorist attack, was essentially numbers.

Shelby now had the numbers she saw permanently stuck in her head. She couldn't get rid of them even if she wanted to. Megan had the decoding software that would help make sense of it all. They needed to put together Shelby's brain and Megan's computer. And fast. Because whatever the countdown was for was happening about sixty hours from now.

Megan knew about Shelby's dislike of being around people. Driving to DC from Knoxville was too far, so Megan had mentioned her brother-in-law's charter airplane service. The way Shelby saw it, one person in a small airplane was much better than airports and large planes *full* of people. And it was Megan's husband's older brother. That shouldn't be too bad.

So here she was, pulling up to a restaurant based on a text message she'd received from somebody named Chantelle DiMuzio, personal assistant of Dennis Burgamy. The assistant had requested that Shelby call Burgamy, but Shelby couldn't remember the last time she'd used her phone to *talk* into. Her outgoing voice-mail message pretty much summed up her opinion about phone conversations:

Sorry, I can't take your call. Please hang up and text me.

Shelby could text much faster than she could talk. She could type twice as fast as that. She was off the charts on a numpad.

Finally, the Chantelle lady had left a message that Mr. Burgamy had arranged for Dylan Branson, Megan's brother-in-law, to meet her at the town's only restaurant. Branson would fly her into DC tonight.

Shelby put the car in Park. Okay. She could do this.

She was already a little shaky from an incident about fifteen miles back when some moron had literally driven her off the road. That was the problem with driving in the mountains: if someone wasn't paying attention—or worse, doing something stupid like texting and driving—and nearly hit you, then it was pretty much game over. These mountain roads with their sheer drops were pretty scary.

It was only because of Shelby's hypervigilance behind the wheel that she'd managed to stay on the road and not drive off the side of the mountain altogether. Shelby wasn't 100 percent sure of her driving skills—she really didn't drive terribly often, and never on roads like these—so she'd wanted to make sure she was paying extra-careful attention.

And thank goodness, because that idiot hadn't even seen her. Didn't slow down, stop, give an "oops, I'm sorry" wave or anything. Shelby could've been flipped upside down at the bottom of the ravine right now and she doubted the other driver would've even noticed. He, or she, just sped on.

So, all in all, not a great start to this adventure. And *adventure* was very much Megan's word, not Shelby's. Shelby's idea of adventure was more along the lines of trying the new Thai place across town, or branching off in a new direction for a video game she was developing. This whole scenario was way beyond *adventure* in Shelby's opinion.

Shelby opened her car door and heard thunder cracking in the darkening sky. Great. More adventure to add to the adventure. Could small planes even take off in a thunderstorm?

Shelby walked to the door of the diner and entered. How would she know who Dylan Branson was? Inside she looked around. There were a couple of middle-aged guys and a woman at the counter, an older lady at the cash register and a teenage waitress carrying food to a couple at a table near the door. Some dark-haired Calvin Klein–looking model sat back in the corner booth—yeah, Shelby *wished* she could be that lucky—and a shorter, stockier man in khakis and a pretty bad polo shirt sat at a table near him.

Nobody was wearing a Trust Me, I'm the Pilot T-shirt or held a sign with her name. So evidently Shelby wasn't going to be able to slip in without having to talk to anyone except Megan's brother-in-law.

Shelby approached the lady at the cash register. "Hi, excuse me—"

"Oh, my goodness. Honey, you're not from around here. I would remember that hair anywhere." The woman's voice wasn't unkind, but it was loud, drawing the attention of pretty much everyone at the diner.

Shelby sighed. Remarks about her hair weren't uncommon. It was red. Not a sweet, gentle auburn, but full-on red: garnet, poppies, wisps-of-fire red—Shelby had heard all the analogies. If she'd been born a few centuries earlier, she would've been burned at the stake as a witch just for her coloring.

Shelby tended to forget how much it grabbed people's attention when they first met her. "Um, yeah. It's really red, I know. I was wondering—"

"You couldn't get that color out of a bottle, I imagine. Especially not with your skin coloring. Your hair must be natural."

See? This was case and point why Shelby tended not to want to talk to people. Because really, did she have to go into her natural coloring with someone she'd known for less than ten seconds? Shelby didn't want to be rude, but neither did she want to talk about which side of the family her coloring was from.

And Shelby was sure that question, or something very similar, would be the next inquiry from the cash register lady.

"Yeah." Shelby remained noncommittal about the hair. "I'm looking for somebody. A pilot. His name is Dylan Branson. He was supposed to meet me here."

"Oh, yeah, honey, he's right over there." The lady gestured toward the corner, and Shelby looked over. Great, it was the balding guy in the bad polo shirt. Shelby thanked her and headed that way before the woman could ask any more questions about her hair.

Dylan Branson was eating what looked like meat loaf at his table and had just put a huge forkful into his mouth when Shelby walked up to him.

"Hi, Dylan Branson, right? I'm Shelby Keelan."

The man looked over at Shelby and his eyes bulged. He held his hand up in front of his mouth, rapidly chewing, and began standing up.

"No, don't get up. I didn't mean to interrupt your meal."

Shelby sat down across from him. Of course, the polite thing for Branson to do would've been to wait until she got there and then eat together, rather than shoveling food in right when he was supposed to meet her. But whatever. Shelby just hoped Megan's husband was a little more considerate than his brother.

And for the sake of her friend, Shelby hoped he was a little more handsome, too. Not balding and portly, like Dylan here. But maybe follically challenged didn't run in the Branson family, just this one brother.

And he was still chewing. How big of a bite could he have taken, for goodness' sake? The look he was giving her over his moving jaw was clearly confused.

"Take your time." Shelby smiled. She didn't want him to choke or anything. That wouldn't get her to DC very quickly.

"Oh, honey, not Tucker," the lady called out from behind the cash register, pointing to the man eating. Then she looked past Shelby to the booth beyond her in the corner. "Dylan Branson, shame on you. You knew this young lady was looking for you. You should've said something."

"I would've, Sally. But I wanted to see if Tucker would actually choke on the meat loaf while trying to talk to her first."

The deep voice came from the booth behind Shelby. She didn't need to look up to see who it was. She knew. The dark-haired, sexy-as-sin Calvin Klein model.

Chapter Three

The attraction punched him in the gut. Dylan had been punched enough times to know clear and well what it felt like: it stole your breath, caused you to wonder which end was up, made your whole body tingle.

Of course, it was usually followed by agony. But in this case it might be worth it.

Striking was the only word for Shelby Keelan. Her red hair fell around her face and shoulders in long wisps and curls that had escaped from the loose braid she seemed to have attempted at some point. Her eyes —now looking at him rather than Tucker—were a clear emerald green with a hint of gold in them.

But, for the love of all things holy, it was her freckles that were killing him. Scattered across her nose, her cheeks, her forehead. They were quite possibly the most alluring thing he had ever seen.

Shelby Keelan wasn't a traditional beauty, but she was striking.

From his corner booth where he could see the main entrance, kitchen entrance and emergency exit—old habits died hard—Dylan had seen her come in. He'd been almost positive who she was from that moment, and then her brief conversation with Sally had confirmed it.

He should've said something when she sat down at the table near his booth and started talking to Tucker, but he couldn't resist seeing how that played out. Poor Tucker still looked as if he was going to have a heart attack.

Shelby Keelan sat in her seat at Tucker's table, her green eyes zeroed in on Dylan. She did not look amused.

"Confused strangers are the top entertainment around here, I take it?"

Uh-oh. Dylan stood, giving Shelby his most charming smile. "Not usually, I promise. I just couldn't resist seeing how Tucker was going to react."

Tucker was still staring at Shelby. "I, uh, I mean, I'm not Dylan Branson." He finally got the words out, much too late to be helpful.

Dylan walked over and slapped Tucker on the back good-naturedly. "I think she caught that much, Tuck. Ms. Keelan is dropping off some items for me to deliver." Dylan looked over at Shelby and held out his hand for her to shake. "I'm Dylan Branson. A pleasure to meet you."

Shelby stood and grasped Dylan's hand. Dylan shook it, then kept it, glad when she didn't snatch it away, and led her over to his booth. "Let's leave Tucker to finish his meat loaf."

A huge crash of thunder shook the windows in Sally's diner. "I can't take off in this anyway. I'll need to let Megan and Sawyer know I'll be delayed for a few hours."

Shelby looked out the window at the rain now pouring down and nodded. "Yeah, that's probably a good idea."

"Maybe you'll let me buy you dinner to make up for my rude behavior. Since we have some extra time before I can fly in this."

Shelby didn't look convinced, but Dylan wasn't going to let it go. The way he saw it, this situation was the best of all worlds: a chance to spend some time with a gorgeous woman, but one who would only be around for a couple of hours. Once the weather cleared and she gave him the codes, they'd go their separate ways. No complications.

But for now he could just enjoy her; her company and her beauty.

"Unless you're in a hurry and just need to drop everything off and run." Dylan gave her another smile. "But I hope that's not the case and you'll have dinner with me."

She gave him a confused look, but then nodded.

"Okay, dinner. A chance to redeem yourself." One of her eyebrows arched as she looked at him.

"Deal. Let me contact Megan and Sawyer to tell them about the storm." Afraid he might yell at Megan for not preparing him for how beautiful Shelby was, Dylan just sent a text to Sawyer.

Shelby in pocket, but storm will delay flight. Will contact with updated ETA soon.

Dylan received a reply just moments later from Sawyer.

Roger that. I'll inform Burgamy.

Good, let Sawyer handle Burgamy. Dylan wanted as little communication time with his ex-boss as possible. He caught the attention of the young waitress who brought them both menus. Shelby began looking through it, but Dylan didn't even need to.

"Already know what you want?" Shelby asked him.

"Yeah. Sally's chicken pot pie is my favorite. I usually get that."

"That sounds good. Perfect for a rainy night and to recover from my near-death experience a little while ago."

As far as Dylan knew, most people didn't have

near-death experiences around Falls Run. He hoped she wasn't talking about poor Tucker. He wasn't *that* bad. "What happened?"

They both ordered pot pie and sweet tea then Shelby told him about the car that had driven her partially off the side of the road. It sounded as if the driver never even saw her.

"Wow, first almost being run off the road, then almost having to have dinner with Tucker. That's a double whammy."

She laughed and relaxed back against the booth. Her eyes sparkled with genuine amusement. Dylan assumed he was forgiven.

"Yeah, the roads around here can be dangerous even for someone who's driven them for years," he continued. "And somebody not paying attention? You're really lucky."

"I thought the same thing after my pulse settled down to something below two hundred beats a minute."

The waitress brought them their iced tea.

"So you and Megan went to college together? Were you close?"

"Well, sort of. Megan was so young when she was at MIT, child prodigy and all that, so she's younger than me. Plus, I'm not a real outgoing person, so I tend to keep to myself. But we banded together a little bit because we were both females in an overwhelmingly large group of men." Shelby took a sip of her tea. "So she married your brother?"

"One of the two, yes. Sawyer. The playboy of the family. It was amazing how fast he fell." Dylan chuckled at the thought.

"And now they have a new baby on the way. I'm happy for Megan. I know back in college she always felt concerned she'd never really fit in anywhere." By the way her face lit up, Dylan could tell Shelby authentically cared for Megan.

The waitress brought their food and they began to eat. "So how many siblings do you have?" Shelby asked between bites.

"I'm thirty-five and the oldest of four kids. Sawyer is the youngest. Cameron is a couple of years younger than me and our sister, Juliet, is sandwiched between Sawyer and Cameron."

"Anybody else married?"

"My other brother, Cameron, to a woman he was involved with a few years ago. They reconnected recently." Dylan didn't mention that Cameron and Sophia had *reconnected* when Cam had taken Sophia hostage while working undercover. That would probably come across as a little weird. "Juliet just got engaged to our longtime family friend Evan. They work together."

Again, mentioning that Juliet and Evan had fallen in love after living through an attack by a crazed stalker probably would be an overshare.

Love in the Branson family tended to be less than traditional.

And that was part of the reason Dylan tried to stay as far as possible from it.

"How about you?" Shelby peeked over her pot pie at him.

"Married once, a long time ago. But not in the cards for me any longer." Dylan definitely did not want to talk about that. "You?"

"Nah. Haven't found anyone yet I like more than my pets."

Dylan laughed. "I don't blame you. Are you a dog person? Please, not cats."

"Both, actually." Shelby smiled at him and began telling him a story about some trouble one of her dogs had gotten into. Dylan matched that story with one of a dog he once had. Soon they were both laughing so hard they could hardly eat.

They were still talking about all sorts of things—her job as a programmer, his as a pilot, her cats that tended to act more like dogs—as they finished their meal, ordered some of Sally's pie and finished that.

Dylan couldn't remember feeling this comfortable and attracted, hell, this *invested*, in a woman in a long time.

He found himself wishing this was more than just a meeting to pick up some data from his sister-in-law's friend. That he and Shelby had more time to spend with each other. But glancing out the window, Sawyer realized the storm would be passing soon. He needed to get the codes to Omega.

The thought of Omega brought all the memories flooding back. All the reasons why Dylan couldn't—*wouldn't*—get involved with another woman.

Tension began to fill Dylan's relaxed body as he realized spending too much time with Shelby was not a good idea. Her smile made him think of things that just weren't in the cards for him. He didn't have it in his heart to love another woman. Burying Fiona and their unborn child, knowing their deaths were his fault, had killed something inside Dylan. He would be wasting time, both his and any woman in his company, by pretending he had anywhere to go in a relationship.

Not that Shelby Keelan had said anything about wanting a relationship with him, for heaven's sake. They were just enjoying a meal together, relaxed conversation. But attraction was fairly crackling between them. Their hands kept touching on the table as they each made some point in a story. He could even feel Shelby's smaller foot next to his leg under the table.

She wasn't being forward, they just had a connection. And Dylan hadn't tried to keep it in check, like he normally would've—not that he'd felt this way about a woman in a long time. Since he'd known he and Shelby would only be together for a couple of hours before she gave him the codes and left, Dylan had deliberately left their natural chemistry unchecked.

He wasn't sure he would've been able to stop it even if he wanted to.

But his plan was backfiring. The more he talked to Shelby, the more he wanted to *keep* talking to her. Her acid wit kept him laughing, her intelligence kept him intrigued, and those freckles…

Those freckles were going to be his undoing. Even right now it was all he could do not to reach across the table and begin kissing a line from one freckle to the next. Starting with the ones on her nose, over to her cheeks and down to the one big one he could see where her jaw met her neck.

He'd have to concentrate on that one especially.

Dylan realized he was inching closer to Shelby across the table and forced himself to lean away, shifting his weight all the way back in the booth, away from her. What the hell was he doing? This was more than mere attraction, it was almost as if Dylan was drawn to Shelby.

Well, that was unacceptable and Dylan needed to get himself under the control he was so well known for. He couldn't believe how close he was to asking Shelby out. To asking her to spend more time with him once he returned from Omega.

Hell, to seeing if she wanted to wait *at his house* for the twelve hours it would take him to deliver the codes to Omega then get home, if he made the round trip as fast as possible.

And that scared the hell out of him.

Shelby wasn't the type of woman Dylan could get involved with. She wasn't a one-night-stand type of girl; that was already obvious. Plus, she was Megan's friend.

He'd let things step over the emotional line with Shelby because they only had a couple of hours. Well, a couple of hours were up. It was time to end this attraction right now. While he still could.

Get the codes. Deliver the codes. Get out.

Shelby was talking about pets. Finishing an entertaining story about how the mama cat had taken a puppy to raise as her own when the puppy's mother had died. Shelby's green eyes had softened while telling it and Dylan had been totally caught up in the story. But now he stopped her, almost abruptly.

"You know, it looks like this storm is making its way out of the area. It's been a pleasure chatting with you, Shelby. But if you'll just give me the codes, I'll be on my way for delivery."

It was rude and came out harsher than Dylan intended. He saw confusion wash over Shelby's face and then self-doubt. Damn it, she was trying to figure out what she had done to initiate Dylan's borderline rudeness. He hated how Shelby drew back and made herself smaller in the booth seat across from him. The smile that had lit her features for almost their entire conversation died.

Dylan hated it, but steeled himself against the apology he found on his lips. It was better this way. Cleaner. But the disappointment in Shelby's eyes actually hurt him. It had been a long time since anything involving a woman had had the power to hurt Dylan. Why should being a jerk to someone he'd only known a couple of hours be able to?

Even if she was the most engaging and fascinating person he'd met in a long time. And the first person who didn't make him want to excuse himself as soon as possible so he could get back to his house, alone.

All of which was just more proof he needed to get away from her as soon as possible.

Dylan could recognize the crookedness of his own logic though he didn't plan to do anything about it. He *couldn't* do anything about it. All he could do was just get away from Shelby before things went any further.

Shelby's brows were furrowed. "Um, I don't understand." Her tone was uncertain.

Dylan rubbed a hand down his face. Damn it, he was making a mess of this. "I think you should just go ahead and give me the codes. Then you can head on back home, or whatever, and I'll take off as soon as I have a chance. All I need is a break in the storms and I'll be fine."

Shelby frowned and shook her head. "But I can't."

"You can't leave Falls Run tonight? Well, there's a motel down the street. I'm sure it's not full." Dylan almost offered to walk her over there, but that was a terrible plan.

Get the codes. Get out.

"No, I mean I can't give you the codes."

"You don't understand, Shelby. It's okay. Megan knows I will deliver them straight to her at Omega. She should've told you I could be trusted, but we can call her so you can talk to her about it yourself. You'll just need to give me the drive, or disk or whatever the codes are on."

"No, *you* don't understand. I can't give you the codes because they're in my head. *I'm* what you're supposed to deliver to Omega Sector."

Chapter Four

You would think she'd just told him she had a nuclear device in her back pocket the way he was acting. Shelby watched from the booth as Dylan went over to pay Sally at the register for their meal.

Shelby tried to think through their conversation to figure out what had happened, where it had gone wrong. Shelby certainly wouldn't be surprised to figure out it was something she had said. It always tended to be something she'd said.

But things had been going so well with Dylan tonight. Laughing and talking with him had been easy. Not full of those awkward pauses that tended to populate Shelby's conversations. Especially ones with really hot guys.

Not that she tended to have too many of those.

Everything seemed to be going great, and then Shelby had watched as Dylan Branson just shut down right in front of her eyes. The light flirting, the laughing, the lack of awkward pauses they had enjoyed the whole evening—totally gone in a split second. The emotional temperature in the room had dropped twenty degrees in just a moment.

Generally, Shelby was always looking for a way to get out of conversations, to find a way to return to her natural solo state. But with Dylan she hadn't felt the need to withdraw. They both seemed to be enjoying the conversation. Enjoying each other. So, yeah, his abrupt termination of *everything* hurt. More than Shelby expected.

Not that she'd been expecting Dylan to ask her to go steady or anything, but they'd been having a good time and then: *pow!* Right in the middle of a sentence he was suddenly finished with her.

See, this was why Shelby avoided people whenever possible.

And then when she told Dylan she had to go with him on the flight? She thought his eyes might bug out of his head.

She hadn't been sure how to respond. When it became clear Dylan wasn't going to elaborate, Shelby had tried to explain. "I have to go. The codes are in my head."

"Well, then write them down or something."

Write them down?

"Do you think Megan and I are idiots?" Shelby asked. "If I could just *write them down*, do you think I would be here with you right now?"

Dylan had shrugged. "I don't know. Maybe."

Shelby had struggled to keep her temper under control. How could this even be the same man she had been talking to so comfortably just ten minutes before? "Well, I wouldn't. If I was able, I would have already used that newfangled thing called the internet to send the codes to Omega. I have to go."

Dylan shook his head. "How big can the codes be if they're in your head?"

Shelby had just sat back and glared at him. "Big."

At that, he stood up, took the bill the waitress had brought a few minutes before and gone over to pay. The restaurant looked to be closing up soon.

Shelby didn't want to explain to him about her photographic memory of anything having to do with numbers. Fifteen minutes ago she wouldn't have minded talking about it, almost had mentioned it when they were discussing her job. But that was when she was talking to good Dylan rather than jerk-face Dylan, who had somehow taken his place. She really wasn't interested in telling him much of anything now.

Maybe Shelby should mention to Megan that schizophrenia might run in her husband's family.

When Dylan didn't immediately return, Shelby looked over at him. Through the window she could see he had stepped outside. He was on the phone now, obviously not happy with whomever he was talking to. Shelby hoped it wasn't Megan.

Shelby also wished she knew what she had done to turn Dylan so hard and cold. Besides just existing and needing a ride. Which was why she was even here. Although that obviously hadn't been explained to Dylan.

Shelby finished her tea as she watched Dylan talking on the phone outside. Another storm had come up and lightning played through the night sky. Shelby didn't think they could take off in all this anyway. Maybe she should drive or look into taking a commercial flight. She could live through being surrounded by all the people at an airport and on an airplane if she had to.

Plus, how much worse could it be than being in an airplane with someone who seemed annoyed by her very existence?

Shelby got up and headed toward the door. She would just go her separate way from Dylan Branson. And hope when she met Megan's husband, Sawyer, that he didn't have the same temperament as his brother.

Shelby opened the door. Dylan's back was to her as he spoke on the phone. "Yeah, I get it. She's needed, too. All I'm saying is that this should've been made more clear to me, Burgamy." Dylan turned around, looking at Shelby while listening to the other person on the phone. "Yes, crystal."

Dylan disconnected the call without saying anything further. Good to know he was gruff with everybody, not just Shelby. They stood for a moment, not saying anything. Lightning flashed around them again.

"Look, I'm not sure what exactly happened here." Shelby gestured toward the inside of the restaurant. "But obviously there was some sort of misunderstanding. You weren't expecting me or whatever. And that's fine. I'm just going to make other travel arrangements."

Dylan rubbed his eyes wearily. "No, that's not going to work. DC is too far to drive."

"I can see about a commercial flight."

"By the time you got to an airport big enough, that would take nearly as long as driving. Listen, I'm sorry I was abrupt before. I just didn't have all the information." Dylan shrugged. "I can fly you to DC. But since this storm seems to have stalled out right on top of us, it's going to be a few hours. Probably three or four."

Four hours? Shelby looked at her watch. It was after 10:00 p.m. She didn't relish the idea of sitting in her car for that long, but surely Sally's diner was going to close soon. Shrugging, Shelby turned toward her car.

Dylan touched her arm. "Look, the airfield is out near my house. Why don't you just come stay at my place, get a few hours of sleep, then we'll be ready to go when this series of storms passes."

Shelby moved away from his touch. "Uh, no, thank you."

"Why?"

"Are you kidding me?" Shelby's voice was pretty loud. A couple leaving the closing diner looked over at Shelby and Dylan. Dylan waved, but Shelby ignored them.

"No, I'm not kidding you. It's a logical solution."

"Why would I stay with someone who out of the blue started treating me like I have the bubonic plague? No, thanks, I'll just stay here."

"You can't stay here. The restaurant is closing." Dylan's voice had raised to a yell, probably to compensate for the thunder overhead. Unfortunately, the teenage waitress came outside just in time to hear his shout, but not the thunder. She stared at Dylan and Shelby with wide eyes.

"Is everything okay, Mr. Dylan?"

"It's fine, Jennifer," Dylan told the girl. "Be careful driving home in this mess."

Jennifer kept watching them as she walked to her car. Looked as if Dylan's yell was the most excitement she had seen in a while.

But the fact that Dylan knew Jennifer's name reassured Shelby a bit, as did the fact that the girl was so shocked by how he was acting. Obviously,

Dylan didn't normally stand around the parking lot yelling at women.

"Sally is closing up for the night. You can't go back in there."

"Fine. I'll just hang out in my car. Text me when you think it's safe to take off and I'll meet you at the airport."

Shelby heard Dylan's sigh. "It's not an airport, more like an airfield." A few drops of rain started to fall. It wouldn't be long until the thunderous clouds produced rainstorms again.

"Don't stay in your car," he continued. "There's a motel a couple of blocks down the road. Stay there at least. Not out in this storm."

He was right. Shelby didn't mind paying for a room she'd only spend a few hours in. Especially if it meant she wouldn't have to talk to any other people unnecessarily.

Or have to stay with a man who had made up his mind to dislike her for no apparent reason.

Shelby left the shelter of the overhang near the diner's front entrance to cross to where her car was parked. "Okay, fine." She gave him her phone number. "Just text me or whatever when you're ready."

The rain was really starting to come down now. "I'll follow you in my truck. Just to make sure everything's okay."

That was the exact opposite of what Shelby

expected. She said nothing, just pulled up the collar of her jacket for protection from the rain. She thought she heard Dylan say something else to her, but she just wanted to make it across the street to her car. She understood why they had built the restaurant on one side of the road and the parking lot on the other—the diner had amazing views of the Blue Ridge Mountains. They wouldn't want to use any of that prime real estate on parking.

But having to cross the street in the rain made Shelby wish they had put the parking closer.

She heard someone yell, but figured it was someone from the restaurant saying goodbye to Dylan. If he was trying to get her attention, he could just wait until they got to the motel. She wasn't having a conversation out in the cold rain.

Shelby heard the squealing of tires as she reached the other side of the road. She looked up to see a car barreling toward her so fast she couldn't even figure out what to do.

Her world tilted as a weight hit her from her right and she went flying sideways through the air. A split second later, the car sped through where Shelby had just been standing, not even slowing down. It sprayed water from puddles, soaking Shelby from head to foot.

From where she lay on the ground, Shelby sucked in deep breaths, trying to get her bearings. She'd been hit, right? But not by the car. She turned her head to the side and saw Dylan lying on the ground with her.

"Are you okay?" he asked.

"Yes. Are you? What in the world just happened?" Her limbs were tangled with Dylan's.

"That car almost hit you. I saw it speeding down the road and yelled, but you didn't hear me."

That wasn't totally true. Shelby had heard him, she just hadn't wanted to stop in the rain.

"Well, your reflexes are better than mine. Thank you."

"I had forward momentum going for me, otherwise I wouldn't have made it."

What he really meant was *Shelby* wouldn't have made it. Dylan could've stayed safely on the side of the road and would've been just fine.

They both began to sit up. Ouch. Shelby could already feel a rip in her coat at the elbow where she'd hit the hardest, although Dylan had taken the brunt of the fall.

"Are you okay?" she asked him. "You took your weight and some of mine."

"Yeah, I'll be fine." Dylan got to his feet then offered his hand to help Shelby up. She gratefully took it, grabbing her purse and working her way to a standing position. Now everything was starting to hurt. And this was what *not* getting hit by a car felt like.

"Did the person driving just not see me?" They walked the rest of the way to her car.

"It's possible."

"But?" Shelby could hear the but in his tone. She was trying to get her keys out of her purse, but found her hands were shaking pretty badly. Dylan reached over and held the purse for her so she could manage to fish them out.

"But it actually sped up. Definitely wasn't typical rainy-night-driving behavior."

"Drunk, I'll bet you. That's the second time I've been almost run off the road. People around here need to pay better attention." Shelby got her keys out and clicked open her car. She just wanted to get out of the rain.

Dylan was looking toward where the car had sped off. "Yeah. For sure."

They walked together around to her driver's side. He held the door open as she got into the car then shut it. Shelby cracked the window so she could hear what he had to say.

"The motel is just a couple blocks down on the right. Don't go anywhere else, okay? Just check in and rest until I let you know we can take off."

Shelby nodded. She wasn't planning on doing anything but taking a hot shower and changing into dry clothes.

"I won't. I don't think I'm up for much dancing."

A hint of a smile formed at Dylan's mouth.

"You'd be hard pressed to find dancing around here anyway. Unless they've got the karaoke set up at the Blue Moon, Falls Run's bar."

The rain was pouring over Dylan. Shelby kind of felt bad for all the mean things she had thought about him since he'd saved her life and all. "Are you sure you're okay?" she asked him.

"Fine. Bye."

Evidently, gruff Dylan was back.

"Okay, let me know when it's time to go." Shelby rolled up her window and started driving slowly down the road, not even looking back at Dylan in the rearview mirror. She was irritated at him and her whole body ached.

This was why she tried to stay alone in her house as much as possible.

Chapter Five

Somebody was trying to kill Shelby Keelan.

Dylan hadn't wanted to say that to her in the parking lot of Sally's diner while they were both soaking wet and banged up by a hard fall to the asphalt. Although, there probably wasn't ever a good time to tell someone their life was in jeopardy.

And Shelby's was. By someone who was trying to make it look like an accident. The car that nearly ran Shelby down hadn't been a drunk driver. As a matter of fact, it had probably been the same vehicle that had nearly driven her off the road earlier today. Both attempts had failed, but just barely.

Dylan walked to his truck, opened it and hopped in, whistling through his teeth as he made it into the cab. Had he cracked a rib again? Damn it, he hoped not. Those hurt like hell. At the very least, his ribs were bruised. His shoulder, too. It had taken the brunt of the fall. But he was in one piece and so was Shelby.

He'd almost been too late. If he'd reacted two seconds later, or if he hadn't trusted his gut that told him that car was trouble, Shelby would be dead. No one could've survived being hit at that speed.

Dylan hadn't gotten any info about the car that would help them. Four-door, dark sedan wouldn't narrow down anything; it wasn't even worth calling in. And the car had been speeding by too fast for Dylan to catch helpful details.

Dylan watched as Shelby pulled out of the parking lot and began driving slowly down the street. He started his truck so he could follow her. He'd make sure she got safely inside, then would try to go get some sleep himself for a couple hours. Surely she would be safe at the motel.

But there had already been two attempts on her life. What would stop whoever was behind this from coming back to finish her in her motel room? That might actually be easier.

Dylan knew he needed to get her to come stay at his house. Dylan wasn't connected to her in any known way, so whoever was following her wouldn't be looking for her at his house. She could leave her car parked at the motel and Dylan could sneak her out the back door in case someone was watching.

Of course, he'd have to stop acting like a total jerk if he wanted to convince her to do that. How had Shelby phrased it? Treating her as if she had the plague.

Dylan ran a weary hand over his face as he parked his truck across the street from the motel and watched Shelby walk into the front office. Yeah, he definitely could've handled that whole situation at the restaurant better. But he'd thought Shelby would just give him the codes and they'd go their separate ways. She might think he was a little abrupt, but no real harm done.

How the heck was Dylan supposed to have known the codes were in her head and that she needed to be at Omega for all of this to work? How was that even possible? If the number sequence was too lengthy to be written up or easily transferred by an electronic medium, then how the hell could Shelby Keelan have them all inside her brain?

When his ex-boss had called, Burgamy should've made it abundantly clear that Shelby would be coming with Dylan to Omega HQ. Dylan had mentioned that fact to Burgamy, who had just quipped back: What difference does it make? Your plane seats more than one, right? You can fit some codes and one woman.

Yeah, his Cessna sat more than one—up to eight, in fact—but that wasn't really the point.

Dylan would've kept much more of a distance from Shelby if he had known they would be together for a few days.

Because Dylan wasn't sure he could keep his hands off Shelby Keelan for days. He hadn't felt this attracted to anyone in a long time. Not since Fiona. Hell, maybe not even *for* Fiona.

Which he couldn't even bring himself to think about.

There had been women since Fiona, of course. During the beginning downward spiral, there had been way too many women—just part of a series of bad choices Dylan made in the name of dealing with unbearable grief. But none of them had meant anything; none of them had touched him in any sort of meaningful way.

After just a few short hours in Shelby's company, Dylan wasn't sure he'd be able to say the same thing about her.

Dylan wasn't proud of how he'd handled the situation at the diner. A yelling match in front of Sally's was never a good plan. But the thought of spending more time with Shelby? It was both the most exciting and most frightening prospect Dylan had had in his personal life in years.

And now Dylan had to talk her into coming to his house. Her presence there, even for only a few short hours, was going to disrupt his peaceful, orderly life. Dylan just knew it. But what other choice did he have? He couldn't leave her in town alone. So even though she didn't seem too keen on the idea of staying with him, Dylan would have to change her mind.

And he would just have to keep the attraction he had for this woman, and her damn freckles, under control.

From across the street, Dylan watched as Shelby came back out of the motel's office, key in hand. She drove her car a little farther into the parking lot and parked in front of a room. After a moment, she got out of her car with a small suitcase and entered her room.

The Falls Run Motel wasn't fancy, but it was clean and family friendly. There was one building with two floors of rooms. The back of all the bottom-level rooms had sliding glass doors with small concrete patios; the upper-level rooms all had small decks, both providing views of the mountains.

Shelby's room was on the first floor, which made Dylan's plan much easier. He had to talk to her, but knew he didn't want to go through her room's front door. He needed to get her out in secret in case someone was watching. That left the back sliding glass door.

Dylan pulled his truck farther into the shadows of the bank parking lot that stood across the street from the motel. He turned off the engine and flipped a switch for the light in the cab so it wouldn't turn on when he opened the door. Just in case. He slid out of the cab, pushing all pain to the side. He felt a little ridiculous hugging the shadows as he made his way across the street in the rain, but he'd learned over the years that an ounce of prevention was worth three and a half tons of cure.

Dylan made his way around the back of the motel, keeping away from the lights. He silently walked along the line of trees until he was right behind Shelby's room. No lights were on in the rooms on either side of her, which was good. Shelby had pulled the curtain closed, so only a tiny bit of light cracked through the glass door. Dylan approached the door and tapped on it softly.

"Shelby." Dylan put his mouth almost up to the door. He didn't want his voice to carry. He could see the shadow of movement in the room, but couldn't tell if Shelby could hear him. He tapped again, a little louder.

The curtain inched back and Shelby peeked out, but Dylan could tell she still couldn't see him from where he was in the shadows. He tapped again right where she was looking and brought his face close to the window.

Her short shriek made Dylan thankful there wasn't anyone in the rooms next to hers. The curtain flew back down, but Dylan heard the unlocking of the door a moment later.

"You scared the pants off me," Shelby hissed. She had a towel wrapped around her neck, drying rain out of her long red hair. It looked even more red against the white of the cloth.

"Sorry."

"What are you doing here? And why are you at the back door? Why didn't you use the front?"

Dylan put a finger up to his lips. He didn't want her to announce to everyone he was here. "I'm trying to talk with you without anyone knowing I'm here. Do you mind if I come in?"

At least she didn't hesitate as she opened the door farther and stepped back, which surprised Dylan a little bit. He wouldn't have been surprised if he had to plead his case from a cracked door after how he'd acted. He walked in and slid the door closed behind him, pulling the curtain to give them privacy from any possible prying eyes.

"Come back because you found just the right words to let me know how you don't like me?" Shelby stood, arms folded and eyebrow raised, by one of the beds in the room.

Dylan winced. He supposed he deserved that, at least a little.

"I'm sorry about before."

If anything, Shelby's eyebrow arched even higher. She didn't say anything.

"Listen, I was going to leave you alone here, let you get some rest, go home and do the same myself before we leave in a couple hours. But the fact is, someone tried to kill you tonight."

Shelby looked shocked then sat down on the bed and began smoothing her wet hair with the towel almost absently. "First of all, thanks for saving my life. But me almost dying and someone trying to kill me are two different things, Dylan."

"I know. I don't use the terms interchangeably." Dylan took a step closer, more to keep his shadow away from the curtain than anything else. But his action drew her attention. She stood and began walking farther away without a word, turning her back to him.

Dylan sighed. He guessed he deserved that, too.

But instead of taking the plastic chair at the farthest point away from him in the room, as Dylan thought she was going to do, Shelby walked into the bathroom and came back out with another towel a moment later. She tossed it to him and sat back down on the bed.

"You look as miserable as I feel. Maybe that will help dry you off enough so that you're at least not dripping."

Dylan began to towel off his face and hair. "Thanks."

"Don't look so surprised. I'm not a she devil, you know."

"I never thought you were."

Her eyebrow rose again.

Dylan changed the subject. "That guy tonight wasn't a drunk driver who got sloppy. That car was someone coming at you with the specific intention of running you down."

Shelby stopped drying her hair and clutched the towel to her like a security blanket. Her green eyes were huge in her pale face. "Do you really think that's true?"

"Well, let me ask you this. Do you remember anything about the car that almost ran you off the road earlier today while you were driving up here?"

Shelby shrugged. "Not too much. I'm good with remembering numbers, but not much of anything else."

Dylan didn't want to just feed an image into her mind. He wanted to see if he could help her remember. "Was it a light or dark color, or maybe a specific color you remember, like red or yellow?"

"No, definitely not a bright color. It was dark, maybe black or gray. I can't really recall."

"That's okay." Dylan sat down on the bed across from hers. "Is there anything you can remember about the model of the vehicle? Maybe it was an SUV or a noticeable brand of car, like a VW or a Jeep?"

"No, I don't know anything about cars. But it

wasn't anything like that. I just remember thinking it was an old person's car. That maybe it was some old person who shouldn't be driving at all if he or she was going to run people off the road."

"Okay, an old person's car." That was the info Dylan had been hoping for. "A sedan."

"Yeah, a sedan." Shelby nodded. "But I don't know what make or anything."

"That's okay, you don't have to. But I think you might find it interesting that the car that tried to run you down tonight was also a dark sedan. Someone has tried to kill you today. Twice. Both in ways that would seem like an accident."

Shelby bounded off the bed. The towel was still clutched in front of her. "What am I going to do?"

"I don't think it's safe for you to stay here tonight in case that person tries to come back and finish what he started. It would be too easy to find you."

Shelby nodded almost blankly.

"I know you were pretty resistant to this idea before, but I think you should come back to my house. Nobody would know you're there and we'll leave in the plane as soon as possible. It's not safe for you to be alone anymore."

Chapter Six

Shelby could hear what Dylan was saying, but it was as if she was processing it too slowly to make sense. Someone was trying to kill her? On purpose?

The whole concept was pretty foreign. And Dylan was afraid someone would find her here at the motel?

"How would they find me here?" she asked.

"It's the only motel in all of Falls Run. If you assumed that what happened earlier was only an accident, you'd probably check in here, get some rest. If I was a killer, I'd look here first."

Shelby walked over by the curtains. She wanted to peek out, to open the door and see if the boogeyman was on the porch ready to attack them, but knew she couldn't.

Was Dylan right? Could someone actually be trying to kill her? They were dealing with DS-13, which Megan assured Shelby was definitely a group to take seriously. Shelby had the codes in her head and knew the numbers were some sort of countdown. But she had no idea what they were counting down to; that's where Megan's computer decryption program came in. Shelby and Megan's computer program had to be in the same room together so Shelby could feed in the data and eliminate what wasn't necessary. Only Shelby could do that. And once she did, they'd be able to figure out the what and the where the countdown referred to.

Were the numbers in her head worth someone killing her for? She didn't want to think so, but the aches and bruises from her close encounter with a speeding car—which did look a lot like the one she'd seen earlier today, now that Dylan mentioned it—told her otherwise. So, yeah, maybe someone was trying to kill her.

Yet another reason why she should have just stayed home.

At least Dylan didn't seem so irritated by her very existence anymore. He wasn't the sexy, flirty Dylan he'd been a few hours ago, but at least he wasn't yelling at her. She didn't necessarily want to go back to his house with him, but neither did she want to stay here with a possible attacker. Uncomfortable was definitely better than dead.

She nodded at Dylan. "Okay, I'll come with you."

Dylan tossed the towel down on the bed. "Good. That really is the safest thing."

"Should I bring my whole suitcase? Everything I brought?"

"If you need everything, I can carry the whole suitcase out. But it would be better if you had just a small bag with a few necessities. Makes us much more mobile getting to my truck."

"Okay."

"Plus, if someone does break in here, it makes it look like you're still around somewhere. It would cause the perp to think maybe he missed you somehow. Buy us more time while he waits for you to come back."

Shelby shuddered at the thought of someone coming in here, waiting for her. She looked quickly at the front door and the glass door. Two ways someone could get in. Shelby definitely didn't want to stay here.

"Let me pack a bag." Shelby grabbed a shirt, a pair of jeans and some underwear, rolling them into a ball with the delicates—did it have to be a red-and-black thong?—on the inside. Shelby grabbed a toothbrush and a comb, thankful she'd never been one for wearing much makeup. The tennis shoes and socks on her feet would be fine.

This should be all she needed. The rest she could buy once she got to Washington, DC.

"I don't have anything to put this in," Shelby told Dylan.

"That's okay. I've got a small duffel bag you can use once we get to my house. Just put your comb and toothbrush in your back pocket and ball up your clothes."

Shelby did as he said. "Are we going to need to run?"

"We will at first, out to the tree line behind the motel. There's no way around that. We've got to get away from the building as quickly as possible. But otherwise, I hope not. Two people sprinting across the street draws a lot more attention than two people just walking fast to get out of the rain." Dylan looked around the room. "You don't have a baseball cap or hoodie, do you? Anything with a hood?"

"No."

Dylan shrugged. "Your red hair is hard to hide without something covering it. Just stay as close to me as you can as we're crossing the street. If I stop, you stop. Don't ask questions, just do it."

Shelby wasn't planning on asking for justification for everything he did while he was getting them out of here. It would be nice if he would take her for a little bit less of an idiot. "Fine."

If Dylan noticed Shelby's annoyance, he didn't mention it. He walked over to the front door and turned off the lights in the room, plunging it into darkness.

"Let's give our eyes a chance to adjust. Then we'll head out."

Shelby nodded then realized he couldn't see her. "Okay."

After a few moments, Shelby's vision adjusted. Dylan had made his way over to the sliding glass door already and was peering around the curtain.

"Is somebody out there?" Shelby asked after what seemed like a long time.

"Probably not. Whoever wants to hurt you would probably come through the front door. Most motel rooms don't have doors at the back, just windows that don't open. Unless he's familiar with this motel specifically, then he'd think the front door was the best bet."

"Oh." Shelby couldn't think of anything more intelligent to say. How did Dylan, a pilot, know all that? Maybe he sat around and watched too many crime shows on television.

"Are you ready?"

Shelby took a deep breath. "Yes."

"Okay, Freckles. Remember, stay as close to me as possible and try not to talk."

Did he just call her Freckles? Shelby didn't even have time to get offended. Dylan was already out the door. She followed him quickly, clothes tucked under her arm, sliding the door shut on her way out.

Dylan made a dash for the tree line, a hundred feet or so from the hotel. Shelby made sure to keep up with him. Once they were in the cover of the trees, Dylan stopped for a minute.

"Okay?" he asked her.

"Yeah."

"We'll make our way along the trees to the side of the motel by the office, then we'll cut across the street. My truck is parked at the bank."

They made their way silently along the trees, keeping to the shadows as much as possible. Dylan kept hold of the hand Shelby wasn't using to carry the clothes, keeping her close to his side. Every once in a while Dylan would stop and peer out. Shelby forced herself not to ask what he saw, if anything.

When they reached the side of the motel, the trees stopped. They'd have to walk out in the open now. Shelby peeked around Dylan's large shoulders. As far as she could tell, nobody was out. Why would they be? Anyone with any sense was inside, not outside in the wet cold. Shelby shivered.

"Are you ready?" Dylan asked, turning his head back toward her so she could hear him over the rain. "We'll walk side by side to my truck. I don't see anybody, but don't dawdle."

Shelby nodded and Dylan took her hand and they began to walk through the parking lot and across the street. Compared to the cover of the trees, Shelby felt exposed out in the open. She kept her head tucked down and walked as quickly as possible, but the steps across the street seemed to take forever.

When Dylan slowed down and curved Shelby into the crook of his arm, Shelby glanced up. She knew he wouldn't choose now to turn this into a lover's pose unless he had to.

"What?" she asked him.

"A car just turned onto the road up the block. A sedan."

"The same one?"

"I don't know, but I don't want to take any chances. I need to keep you out of sight and away from anything that might associate you with me." Dylan turned them away from where his truck was parked. "Detour."

Shelby kept up as Dylan now rushed across the street toward the bank building rather than his vehicle. He didn't stop until they were standing up against the wall of the bank, the opposite side from where the car was coming. Shelby clutched her balled-up change of clothes to her chest with one arm.

"Okay, we're going to work our way around

to the back side of the building and see what that car is doing."

They stayed against the wall as they walked back. Dylan had yet to let go of Shelby's hand. When they got to the back where they could glance out to see the road, Shelby stayed behind Dylan while he took a look.

"I don't see anybody. Maybe that car wasn't even the same guy."

"That's good, right?"

Dylan nodded and let go of her hand. Everything seemed safe. Shelby wondered if this whole thing was just a case of overactive imaginations. Admittedly, it was unlikely that two cars similar in make and model would almost hit her twice in one day, but it wasn't impossible.

"Okay, I don't see anyone," Dylan told her again. "Let's head to the truck."

Shelby nodded and they began walking, neither of them quite as worried about secrecy.

Shelby felt Dylan stiffen a moment before she noticed the car again herself. It was pulling out of the parking lot directly adjacent to the bank, moving slowly, obviously looking for something or someone.

Okay, maybe not overactive imaginations.

Dylan grabbed Shelby's hand again and pulled her forward, then put his other hand on her head to get her to stay low. They ran to his truck, keeping as low as possible. Dylan opened the passenger-side door and jumped in, sliding across the seat and reaching to help Shelby at the same time.

"Hurry. Stay down." Dylan's voice was curt as he kept a watchful eye out the windshield while trying to stay out of sight himself. Shelby threw her clothes toward him, grabbed his hand and climbed. She pulled the door closed as quickly as she could, glad that no lights had come on in the cab. She ducked down low in the seat.

"Is he still coming toward us?"

"Yes, but I don't think he saw us. It looks more like a sweep-through than anything. He's past us now."

Shelby peeked up and saw the rear of the car as it drove slowly by. The person driving was looking for someplace. Or someone. But the car was moving on now.

Dylan straightened up in his seat. "I think it's safe now. But let's get out of here before he comes back. Once he's sure the street is clear, he'll try to find you at your room."

"Okay." Shelby sat up and reached to grab her clothes which had fallen all over the cab when she'd thrown them inside. She found her pants and shirt with no problem. But kept feeling around the darkened cab for her underwear.

"Um, I think this is what you're looking for."

Hanging from Dylan's finger was Shelby's black-and-red lace thong.

Chapter Seven

Dylan didn't allow himself to dwell on that tiny scrap of lace during the drive to his house. He needed to stay focused and make sure no one was following them. Although he knew following them on the windy road that led from town to his house with no headlights would be nearly impossible.

But that gave him too much time to think about red-and-black material, so he focused instead on being doubly sure no one followed.

No one did.

The storm still raged as they reached Dylan's house fifteen minutes later. Although he normally wouldn't park there, he pulled into the garage so they wouldn't have to get wet again. Shelby was just beginning to stop shivering. She hadn't said much of anything on the drive here. Once she'd snatched the thong off his finger, she'd kind of hunkered down over on the opposite side of the cab.

About as far from Dylan as she could get.

Dylan turned off the ignition and opened his door. He would've gone around to help Shelby, but she'd already made it out fine on her own. So he opened the door that led through a small mudroom before entering the main part of his house.

Dylan's house wasn't too large. Three decent-size bedrooms, a living room with a large fireplace and a kitchen with an eat-in nook. Dylan had designed and built most of it himself, based on his own needs and preferences. It definitely had not been built with entertaining in mind. Hell, except for family, Dylan never entertained anybody at his house. Any meetings concerning his charter business were conducted at his office by the airfield a half mile away.

Dylan wasn't a sloppy person—his mother hadn't allowed it growing up, neither had the army—but still he looked over his house with a critical eye. He'd never brought a woman here before, and for the first time had a moment's doubt. What did his house look like to Shelby? Too sparse, too masculine, too rough around the edges? There definitely weren't a tremendous amount of creature comforts here.

Dylan wondered if Shelby would start complaining right off the bat, or if she'd be too polite to do so. She hadn't seemed to hold back any of her opinions so far, so Dylan didn't expect her to do so now. But when he turned to look at Shelby as she walked farther into the living room, she didn't seem to be put off at all by his house.

"This is a great space," she told him, looking around. "Lots of windows. I'm sure that lets in great light during the day."

Dylan had to admit he was impressed. He didn't think Shelby would notice the windows, his favorite feature, first. He thought she might notice the kitchen was small and rather rustic—Dylan wasn't much of a cook—or that the television was pretty tiny in the living room and off to the side.

"I like the feeling of trees around me. The windows help almost bring them indoors." Dylan walked over and moved a book that lay open on the couch cushion and put it on the stack of books already on the end table. "Do you want to sit down? Or do you want to rest? As soon as this storm breaks we need to take off."

"How far is your airplane from here?"

"Less than a mile. There is a stretch of flat area and I built a runway, not a big one, but big enough for my Cessna. The hangar and my office are up there, too."

Shelby was still clutching her bundle of clothes. "I guess I'll rest. It's getting pretty late. Can we take off in the dark?"

"Yeah, dark is fine. Just not in the storm." It

was almost midnight now. Dylan estimated they'd be able to take off in about three hours.

He led the way down the hall. "The guest room is right here." He opened the door and turned on the light, then winced. He'd forgotten that he had piled his book collection on the guest bed until he could get around to building the new bookshelf he wanted.

Shelby walked in and crossed to the bed. "Looks like my bed space is already taken up by Zane Grey and Louis L'Amour. Although I think I'm seeing a little C. S. Lewis in there, too. Pretty extensive collection."

"I'm sorry. Look, I can get this cleaned off in just a minute." Dylan grabbed a stack of books and began moving them across the room, but Shelby touched his arm.

"Dylan, it's fine. Just leave them. If you've got a blanket and a pillow, I'll just sleep out on that giant couch you have."

Dylan hesitated. Was that rude? He'd lived alone for too long. He didn't want to deliberately alienate Shelby; he'd done enough of that already this evening.

Shelby ended up answering the question for him. "Truly, it's okay. We've only got a couple of hours. No point using a chunk of that cleaning off a bed. Just hand me a towel so I can take a shower, and dump a pillow and blanket on the couch."

She was right, it would take him twenty minutes to clean off this bed enough that someone could sleep on it. Maybe he should offer her his bed.

No. Dylan had the feeling if he let Shelby sleep in his bed he'd never stop thinking about her there. "Okay, I'll get you a towel. Sorry about this."

Dylan got her what she needed and showed her to the guest bathroom. He went in there before her to check the status of the tub. It was pretty dusty—the whole room was pretty dusty; Dylan didn't get in there much—but it was relatively clean and usable.

"I'll leave a couple of blankets and pillows on the couch. Try to get a little rest. As soon as the storm breaks, we'll head out." Dylan closed the door behind him without looking at Shelby again.

Dylan took the items Shelby would need to sleep and placed them on the couch, then walked into his bedroom. He needed to try to catch a little sleep himself. But he could hear the shower running in the guest bathroom.

He definitely was not going to get any sleep thinking about Shelby, and her adorable freckles, in the shower. Or the never-to-be-mentioned black-and-red thong sliding onto her body afterward. Dylan needed a shower himself.

A cold one.

SHELBY LAY ON the couch looking up at the high ceiling of Dylan's house. Here, under blankets that weren't hers, on a couch that wasn't nearly as comfortable as her own bed, in a house she wasn't familiar with, Shelby knew she should be freaking out.

She did not do well out of her own house for very long. And although she had prepared herself to go to Washington, DC, Shelby had thought she would be staying with Megan. An old friend. A *safe* friend who understood Shelby's need to be alone after a time in other people's company.

Instead, she was at the house of a man who constantly made her either want to slap him or kiss him. He was definitely not safe, the opposite, in fact. And yet she was here in his house, quite comfortable.

Shelby wasn't freaking out at all.

As a matter of fact, she was a little freaked out that she wasn't freaking out. She kept preparing a speech in her mind that she would use on herself when the panic came.

But it didn't come.

Shelby wasn't just under the blankets, she was *snuggled* under the blankets. And looking up at the tall rafters of Dylan's ceiling, she found the space and the openness…calming.

Shelby had been called a lot of things in her life, but calm was not one of them. She liked things to be the way she wanted them. Her house was exactly the way she liked it, everything had its place and Shelby knew where that place was. She'd lived in her downtown Knoxville condo, right smack in the heart of the city, with views of World's Fair Park and the Sunsphere, for over eight years, and she loved it. In all that time, she'd never felt comfortable anywhere else. She liked the constant sound of traffic right outside her windows, and even the noise of neighbors in the building.

So Shelby couldn't quite figure out how she felt so comfortable lying here in the gentle peace of the mountains surrounding Dylan's cabin. But she wouldn't question it anymore. She'd just rest. She didn't think she would be able to sleep. Resting was one thing, but sleeping would be something totally different. She didn't sleep in strange houses. In fact, she hadn't been able to get a full night of sleep outside of her own bed in years. But she could rest.

The next thing Shelby knew, Dylan was gently shaking her shoulder to wake her up.

"Hey, there's a break in the storms. Time to head out."

Shelby opened her eyes to find Dylan crouched down beside her.

"Okay, I'm not asleep, just resting."

Dylan snickered at that.

"What?" Shelby demanded.

"Well, for somebody just resting, you had the most adorable little snores coming out of you." Dylan stood up and began walking into the kitchen.

"I do not snore." Wait, did she? It wasn't as if there had been anyone around to let her know about her sleep-breathing patterns in a long time. But Shelby was pretty sure she didn't snore. Plus, she hadn't been sleeping. Shelby sat up on the couch. Had she been sleeping?

No, because that would mean she had been comfortable enough to sleep at Dylan's house. So, no, she hadn't been sleeping.

Shelby looked over to where Dylan was fixing coffee and breakfast in the kitchen. "What time is it?"

"Almost four o'clock."

Over three hours since she'd lain down. She *had* been sleeping.

"I do not snore," Shelby muttered again under her breath as she got up and began folding the blankets she'd slept on. She didn't want to think about sleeping or not sleeping.

"Coffee?" Dylan asked from the kitchen. "And I have breakfast. Not much, though. Toast, cereal. And I have some yogurt."

"Coffee, please." Shelby shuffled into the kitchen. Although she felt better after her...*rest*, she could still use some caffeine. She sipped it gratefully after Dylan poured her a mug.

"As soon as you're ready, we'll head up to the airstrip. It looks like we have about a forty-five-minute window before the next storm set moves in."

"Okay." Shelby nodded, sipping her coffee faster. "I'll hurry."

"You can bring breakfast with you. I'll need to do a quick preflight check on the plane, and you can eat in the hangar."

Dylan was all business, but was at least being pretty friendly. As friendly as a person could be when it was four o'clock in the morning and your day was already starting. Shelby finished her coffee and grabbed what she wanted for breakfast to take with her. She ran into the bathroom to comb out and braid her hair and brush her teeth with the toothbrush and comb that had survived the trip from the hotel. Dylan had given her a small bag, so she put last night's clothes in there.

The drive to the airstrip didn't take long. It still drizzled outside, but there wasn't any thunder and lightning. Shelby waited in Dylan's truck, parked in the hangar behind his plane, as he ran through his preflight checklist.

This was a pretty nice setup he had here. The airstrip was on his land, and it was only his plane that took off or landed, so Air Traffic Control wasn't a problem. The only problem, Shelby was sure, had been getting an area flat enough and safe enough for a plane to take off around here, surrounded by the Blue Ridge Mountains. But Dylan had done it.

She watched him move around his plane with ease, obviously familiar with what he was doing. When his checklist was complete he made his way back over to Shelby and the truck.

"Ready?"

"Yeah."

Dylan helped Shelby out of the truck then grabbed a backpack from the back. Shelby picked up her own small bag of items and walked with him over to the plane. She looked up at the sky. Even through the darkened night, she could still see the clouds, not as thick and threatening as they were before, but still there.

"We're okay with the weather?"

Dylan nodded. "I studied it through some weather sites and FAA reports. We don't have a whole lot of time, but we have enough."

Dylan helped Shelby up the stairs of the plane, entering behind her. She shifted to the side so he could pull up the stairs and close the door, securing then double checking it.

"Trust me," he told her, "I wouldn't be taking us up if it wasn't safe."

Dylan's plane was different than Shelby expected. Nicer. As he'd told her, it could fit up to eight people, with two sets of leather seats facing each other across tables and another single row of seats behind them. The setup was a great way to do business or just talk with someone while traveling to a destination.

Shelby turned to Dylan. "Somehow I thought you did more cargo trips than passengers. But you're certainly set up for people."

Dylan walked up to the cockpit. "It's about fifty/fifty right now. Passengers generally pay more, but I prefer cargo if I have the option."

"Oh, yeah? Why is that?"

Dylan gave her a half grin. "Cargo doesn't talk."

Shelby returned his smile. Not wanting groups of talking people? *That* she understood. "Should I stay back here or come up there with you?"

"Either way. The seats recline, so if you want to get some rest, I understand."

Did he want to be alone in the cockpit? Shelby would love to come up there, to see how a plane such as this one really worked, but she didn't want to make a nuisance of herself.

"I'm not going to sleep, but I can stay back here if you'd rather be alone."

Dylan tilted his head a little to the side as if he was weighing the pros and cons. Shelby didn't know whether she should be offended or not.

"Why don't you come up with me? I'm sure that will be more interesting." Dylan turned and walked into the cockpit.

Yeah, Shelby was sure that would be more interesting, too. She followed him.

Dylan handed Shelby a pair of headphones. "These make it easier to talk without having to yell."

Shelby nodded and sat down in the seat next to him. She pulled the headset over her head and adjusted the mic just slightly. Dylan showed her how to buckle in. A harness belt was much different than the ordinary lap belt on most airplanes.

Dylan finished his cockpit preflight checklist quickly, something he'd obviously done hundreds of times. But never did he seem to be rushing. Shelby couldn't help watching him. He was clearly sure of himself and what he was doing. He didn't hesitate, but moved efficiently through the list. Sure, confident.

It was downright sexy.

Shelby decided she better stop staring at him and looked around the cockpit instead. She'd never been in this part of an airplane before. It was exciting.

"Ready?" Dylan asked her. She could hear him without any problem in the headphones.

"Yep. Do I need to do anything?"

"Yes. When I give the signal, stick your arms

out the window and flap them up and down really hard. It helps us to get airborne."

Shelby looked over at him with a grin on her face. Mr. Serious just made a joke. Shelby hadn't been sure he had it in him.

"You just be sure not to hit all the trees around here."

Dylan chuckled slightly. "Actually, the trees at the end of the runway are a concern. Not for us since we're so light today, but with a full load I do have to be aware of them."

Great. She hadn't been nervous, but she was a little now. Shelby hoped Dylan was as adept at flying as he had been prepping the airplane. She sat back and held on to the edges of the seat belts that covered both her shoulders.

The plane built up speed a few moments later and soon they were airborne.

Chapter Eight

Dylan saw Shelby finally release her death grip on the seat belt. He knew that the first time in a cockpit could be a little unnerving to a novice, but now that they were in the air, she seemed to be relaxing a bit.

Dylan still wasn't sure why he had invited her up here with him. Like his house, he considered his Cessna's cockpit to be his own personal space, not to be shared lightly. And yet he'd invited a quirky little redhead into both the places most sacred to him.

Through the lighting of the panels he could see her looking around with wonder in those big green eyes. The sun was just beginning to come up, giving them a little bit more natural visibility.

He wasn't likely to forget the picture she made sitting in the cockpit in the early morning light.

Which was the exact reason why he probably shouldn't have invited her up here.

Dylan looked down at the control panel and the

weather printout he had. They'd have to go out of their way to avoid the storm, but that couldn't be helped. There was no way they were flying through it; that was a risk no good pilot was willing to take if he had any other option.

Dylan waited for questions from Shelby about flying and which buttons and controls did what. Curiosity was only natural from someone in the cockpit for the first time. But although Shelby looked around constantly, she didn't ask any questions. Maybe she just wasn't curious about what he did as a pilot.

For the life of him, Dylan could not figure out why that bothered him.

"No questions?" he asked, growing even more irritated when he found he couldn't keep his irritation out of his voice.

Shelby's look was a little wary. "Actually, lots. But you said 'cargo doesn't talk,' so I figured you preferred quiet. I totally understand."

And just like that, Dylan felt like a total jerk again. She was just doing what he had implied he wanted and he had proceeded to get irritated at her for it.

What the hell was wrong with him? Shelby Keelan twisted him in knots.

"Ask away," he told her. "I promise not to bite."

She smiled just a tiny bit at that. "Honestly, Dylan, you don't have to entertain me. I know what it's like to just want to sit quietly with your own thoughts."

"Well, I appreciate that, but I honestly don't mind your questions."

The sun was beginning to make its way a little bit more over the horizon. They were flying east and soon it would be bright in their eyes. Sawyer reached into his pocket and pulled out his sunglasses and put them on.

"Aviators?" Shelby asked with one eyebrow raised.

"They're called that for a reason. I'll need them a lot in just a minute. There's an extra pair in the Velcro pocket, a little bit behind you to your right."

"How long have you been a pilot?" Shelby asked as she maneuvered around to access the pouch with the glasses.

"I started my charter business almost four years ago. I actually started flying as a helicopter pilot in the army. I got out of the army about ten years ago and went into law enforcement, and also got my private-pilot's license. So I've been flying a long time."

"Something you love?"

Dylan hadn't really ever thought of that question. Did he love flying? "I enjoy the challenge of it, the concentration and control it takes to fly a small jet like my Cessna. I like owning my own business and being able to take the jobs I want."

Shelby nodded. "Yeah, I like that about my job, too."

She developed computer games. She'd talked about that last night.

"How did you get into coding games?" he asked her.

"I'm good with numbers. And at the end of the day, that's what computer coding is—numbers."

"So you're good at your job?"

She shrugged. "I'm the best."

She said it so matter-of-factly you could hardly doubt her. "Is that so? Have you done any games I would've heard of?"

She looked around at the plane's gauges as she answered. Dylan was shocked to hear the names of a couple of the most popular games *in the world* come out of her mouth.

"You developed those games?"

"Yep." Shelby ran her fingers over the air-speed indicator and didn't say anything else.

"Those are really popular games." Dylan wasn't a gamer by any means, but even he had heard of those. They were popular because of the strong female leads, plus parents loved them because they proved games could be addictively challenging and fun without gruesome violence and gratuitous language. But teenagers adored them because of all the add-ons players could download after buying the game. New ones every couple of weeks, unlike other games where you had to wait months or longer.

"Yep." Obviously Shelby wasn't one to brag.

"Did you do all the downloads, too?"

She nodded this time, not saying anything at all.

"You're like a celebrity then, aren't you?"

"Maybe if you're a seventeen-year-old boy with acne."

Shelby would be a celebrity for any seventeen-year-old boy for reasons having nothing to do with gaming, but Dylan kept that thought to himself. "Everybody loved how fast those add-ons came out. Did you do them all?"

Shelby shrugged again. "Yeah."

"How? Not sleeping at all for two years?"

"No, I'm just really quick with numbers and therefore coding. Most programmers have to write, then go back through and see if what they did works on the screen. It's a lot of back-and-forth." Shelby repositioned the sunglasses on her nose as the sun made its way up even brighter. "I have a photographic memory with numbers. So I only have to code things once and know exactly what the results will be."

"And that makes you fast?"

"Really fast. And I don't make any mistakes,

so I don't have to recheck anything like normal programmers."

"You never make a mistake?"

"Not when it comes to numbers. I remember everything about them."

"You're a genius with numbers." It wasn't a question. Dylan already knew it was true. "That's why you went to MIT and that's how you met Megan."

"Megan's the true genius. I just happen to remember digits. But she can figure out, build, tear apart or fix just about anything having to do with computers. It's pretty amazing."

"Yeah, she's helped Omega Sector out on more than one occasion."

"Omega Sector, that's where she works, right? And her husband, Sawyer, too."

"Yeah, actually, all three of my siblings work there."

Shelby nodded. "Is that where you worked when you were in law enforcement?"

Astute little thing, wasn't she? He'd only mentioned law enforcement in passing. "Yes, I worked for Omega for a few years."

"But you quit."

Dylan didn't want to get into this. He wanted to keep Fiona's ghost down on the ground where it belonged, not bring it up here in the cockpit.

"So, you want to fly the plane for a couple of minutes?" he asked her.

Dylan's diversion tactic worked perfectly. Shelby slid her sunglasses down on her nose and looked over at him with big eyes. "Really? Can I? Will we die?"

Dylan chuckled. "I'm pretty sure we won't die. I still have my control column right here in front of me in case I need to take over."

"What do I do?"

Really, at this altitude and since they were just flying straight and not changing direction or speed, she wouldn't be doing much, but Dylan didn't want to say anything that would cause the excitement to fade from her eyes. "You'll just take the yoke right in front of you and hold it steady, and I'll let go."

Shelby reached out for the control column, the plane's steering wheel, that was in front of her chair.

"Then, just try not to do anything to crash us," Dylan continued. Shelby's hands flew back away from the yoke without touching it.

"Wait, what would make us crash?" Dylan winced as she yelled it into the mouthpiece of her headphones.

"I'm just kidding, Shelby. You won't do anything to make us crash." He laughed. "Just keep it steady. Don't pull back or forward quickly and we'll be fine."

She reached over and slapped at his arm, difficult with the harness holding her in. But then she slowly reached out and took the control column.

"I'm going to let go now, okay?"

"Okay." Shelby nodded, but didn't look at him. She had a tight grip on the column.

"Just relax." Dylan let go of the control column, but kept his hands on his knees in case he needed to take back over quickly. "You're flying the plane, Shelby."

"I am?" Shelby glanced quickly over at his hands. "I am," she repeated, wonder clear in her voice this time.

Dylan let her enjoy the moment of realizing she was flying an airplane. She didn't seem in any danger of jerking the steering column.

"Why don't you ease the yoke back toward you just a little bit?"

"That will cause us to go up, right?"

"Yep."

"Don't you have to check with Air Traffic Control or whomever?" Shelby sounded pretty nervous.

"Not to go up just a hundred feet. They allow a little leeway. Plus, there aren't any planes around in the traffic pattern for miles."

"Okay, then. What do I do?"

"Just pull the yoke back toward you, gently and slowly."

The plane began to climb slightly as Shelby did as Dylan instructed. A surprised laugh fell out of her mouth. Dylan grinned.

"Now you're really flying."

Neither of them were expecting the roar and loud popping noise that came from the engine to their right, before it stuttered to silence. Dylan immediately grabbed the control column.

"Oh, no, Dylan, what did I do?" Shelby's voice was frantic.

"That definitely wasn't you, Shelby. That was an engine flameout."

And there was absolutely no reason it should've happened at their rather benign speed and altitude.

"Are you sure?"

Dylan fought to keep the plane steady, more difficult now with only one good engine. They could still fly with just one engine, but they would need to get on the ground soon.

"I'm sure it wasn't you, Shelby. You didn't do anything wrong, I promise."

Dylan needed to call the situation in to Air Traffic Control. Immediately. They needed to get on the ground.

"ATC, this is Cherokee four four six one nine

en route to private UNICOM airfield six two four seven. We've experienced an engine flameout in one engine. Over."

"Roger, Cherokee four four six one nine. You okay? Over."

Dylan looked over at the paper sectional chart then his electronic GPS system. The closest airfield was about sixty miles. They would be able to make it. "Affirmative. Request clearance for set down at unmanned airfield five miles east of Christiansburg. Over."

"Roger that, Cherokee four four six one nine. No traffic reported—"

The Air Traffic Control's words were drowned out by another roar, this time from the left engine. Dylan could see the glare of the flames out of the corner of his eye for a moment before it went out.

Now they were flying with no power in either engine. Shelby's gasp was audible in the silence that now filled the aircraft. There was no way they would make it to that airfield.

"Mayday, mayday, mayday. ATC, this is Cherokee four four six one nine. We have lost the second engine. I repeat, neither engine is responding. Over."

"Roger, Cherokee four four six one nine." Dylan could tell he had the controller's full attention now. "What are your exact coordinates?

Dylan found it hard to look down for the coordinates from the GPS while trying to keep the Cessna under control. They were in essence a glider now. Dylan fought to keep the nose of the plane up.

Dylan glanced over gratefully as Shelby tilted the GPS toward her and read off the coordinates to the air traffic controller.

"Tower, we will be making an emergency landing, location yet undetermined."

"Roger that, Cherokee four four six one nine. We'll contact emergency services in that area."

Dylan looked around for anywhere they could possibly land. The mountains and trees made it difficult. And there was nothing ATC could do to help him now. Dylan didn't know where he would land, so the fire trucks wouldn't know where to go.

"What do we do?" Shelby asked. It was much easier to hear her now with no engine noise.

"We need to find a place to put her down. Fast. Any open area."

It was difficult to see anything around them except trees. He definitely could not land on trees. They were losing altitude quickly. They had only minutes left.

"What about over there?" Shelby pointed to a slight break in the trees maybe two miles away. It wasn't a field, and definitely wasn't a runway, but it was better than the beautiful, but deadly, trees around them everywhere.

Plus, it was the only option. Dylan began to maneuver the plane in that direction.

"C'mon, baby," he muttered as the plane shuddered slightly, resisting his ease toward the opening in the trees.

"Shelby, we're going to be coming down hard and fast. Make sure your harness is on as tightly as possible." Dylan did the same to his own.

The clearing wasn't as large as Dylan had hoped, but they were too low to do anything else now. He slowed the plane as much as possible and prayed they'd live through the next thirty seconds.

The Cessna hit roughly on the top edges of some trees then bounced hard against the ground, flying back up, then coming down roughly again. The impact was bone-jarring, but at least they weren't a ball of flames. Dylan slowed the plane as much as he could and then turned the yoke sharply so the plane began to slide to the side. Working against their own speed snapped them around hard, collapsing one side of the plane as the landing gear gave out, but it slowed them down.

He watched the trees speed toward them and braced himself, hoping he had slowed them down enough not to die in the impact.

He reached out his hand for Shelby, who took it right before they hit the tree line.

Then there was only blackness.

Chapter Nine

Shelby's eyes opened and it took her a minute to get her bearings. She was hanging in the seat sideways, the harness holding her in. The whole cockpit seemed to be tilted at some sort of canted angle.

But she could move all her fingers and toes without much pain and didn't seem to be bleeding. As far as she was concerned, that was the best possible outcome considering what had just happened.

Of course, the whole plane was filled with smoke, so they weren't out of danger yet. She wasn't sure if anything might ignite, but she didn't want to stay around and find out. And she hadn't heard anything at all from Dylan.

"Dylan? Hey, Dylan, are you okay?"

No response. Now Shelby was even more panicked.

"Dylan! Can you hear me?" She struggled to loosen herself from the seat-belt harness, difficult to do when it was supporting a lot of her weight. She finally managed to get the release clasp to function, and fell out of her seat onto the control panel.

She eased her way down to Dylan's seat, where he lay motionless against his belt. Shelby sucked in a panicked breath. Was he dead?

Shelby was reaching to take Dylan's pulse, when he groaned and moved slightly. Oh, thank God. Not dead.

"Dylan? Can you hear me? We're alive. But I think we need to get out of here because there's smoke everywhere."

Shelby braced her legs against the cockpit's small side window, which was now on the ground since the plane was mostly on its side, and used both her hands to ease Dylan's head back from where it hung from the harness. She brushed her fingers through his black hair. "Dylan. Can you wake up? We've got to get out of here."

Maybe she was going to need to get Dylan out on her own. Maybe his injuries were more severe than hers. Shelby began to attempt to unfasten his harness, a feat much more difficult since she couldn't brace his weight with anything. Plus, the fastener seemed to be stuck.

And the smoke was really becoming an issue now. Something was definitely on fire. Not surprising considering they'd just crashed.

Shelby stopped and looked around. *Think*. She needed to get Dylan out of that seat and out of the cockpit, which could turn into a ball of flames at any moment. She needed some sort of knife to cut through his seat belt since she couldn't get it unbuckled.

Hadn't Dylan had some sort of fancy pocketknife earlier? That would be perfect. Which pocket had he kept it in?

Shelby tried to get her hand into one of Dylan's front jean pockets, difficult with how his body was angled in the seat. Shelby tried to force his weight up so she could reach farther into the pocket.

"I think molesting someone while they're unconscious is a crime."

Dylan's deep voice in Shelby's ear caused her to stumble a step backward into the control panel. She felt herself blush. "I, um, was trying to get your pocketknife. I couldn't get your belt to unfasten."

Dylan smiled and pulled at the belt, grunting. "Yeah, I think the clasp is broken. My knife isn't in my pocket, it's in my backpack in the storage compartment behind my seat."

From her stance underneath him, Shelby felt something drip onto her shoulder. She touched the drop with her fingers and saw the red.

"You're bleeding."

Dylan's voice was tight. "Yeah, I think it's my arm. I can feel the burn."

Shelby realized she hadn't even checked to see if Dylan had any injuries. But that would have to wait. She needed to get him out of the harness belt and out of this cockpit.

"Okay, just hang in there. I'm going to get the knife."

The smoke was getting heavier and Shelby was beginning to cough. She maneuvered around until she was behind Dylan's seat, careful not to step on him.

"The storage container is to the left," Dylan told her, coughing between words.

From her vantage point, Shelby could see that the cabin on the plane, although intact, was definitely burning toward the rear. They had to get out of here fast or the fire would block the door.

Shelby found the container and opened it, quickly pulling out the backpack Dylan had stored there, as well as the first-aid kit. "Where's the knife in your backpack?"

"Side pocket." Dylan's voice was noticeably weaker.

Damn it. "Hang on, Dylan. I've got it."

Shelby threw the first-aid kit in the backpack and worked her way back down to Dylan's seat. She got underneath his large chest and pushed up with her arm and shoulder, trying to take some of

Dylan's weight. Once she cut the straps, he was going to fall.

"Ready?" She didn't wait for his response, just opened the knife and sliced through one of the canvas straps at his shoulder, then the other.

There was no way Shelby could hold Dylan once he was released from the belts. He was six foot one of sheer muscle, and probably at least seventy pounds heavier than her. But she did her best to keep him from crashing into the plane instruments below. Although all he really did was just crash into her instead.

She helped Dylan to his feet, a little unsteady herself.

"Okay, let's get out of here," Dylan wheezed, beginning the climb over the pilot seats. He grabbed some sort of map as he was on his way up.

"We have to hurry, there's definitely a fire in the back." Shelby noticed Dylan's arm was bleeding even more now and he didn't look very steady. But he managed to pull himself up and through the flimsy cockpit door that had broken away and into the main cabin, reaching back to help Shelby.

"I'm fine," she told him. "You get the outer door open. I'll get myself out of here."

The outer door was completely blocked because of how the plane lay on its side, but Dylan was able to get the emergency window open. Dylan climbed through, then reached back for Shelby. Both made their way outside, Shelby still carrying the backpack. Smoke poured out of the open window behind them.

They gulped fresh air and stumbled from the wreckage toward the trees. Shelby kept expecting an explosion behind them, but it never came. Finally they sat down against some trees, both of them breathing heavily between coughs. Shelby looked back at the plane. It may not have exploded, but the smoke and fire were now pouring out of it.

It was a miracle she and Dylan were alive at all.

They sat in silence for long moments, both of them trying to catch their breath and process the fact that they had just survived that burning death trap a few hundred yards away.

"So…the landing was a bit bumpy. Sorry about that," Dylan said.

Shelby closed her eyes and began to laugh. "Yeah, maybe if you'd just had a few more flight hours under your belt, it wouldn't have been so rough. Be sure to work on that."

But Shelby knew the truth. If it had been a less capable pilot than Dylan flying the plane, they'd be dead right now. Shelby had no doubt about it.

"What happened up there, Dylan?"

"I don't know, exactly. One engine flaming

out? That can happen. It's highly unlikely, but it can happen. But both engines flaming out? No."

Shelby wasn't sure what that meant. "But both did, right?"

"Yeah, but it wasn't a coincidence. It happened because it was helped along."

"You mean someone sabotaged the plane?"

Dylan nodded. "I thoroughly checked her out before we took off. I take preflight seriously. And there was nothing out of the ordinary to be seen."

"What would have caused the engines to cut off like that?"

"If I had to guess, probably some sort of fuel or oil contamination. It ate away at the integrity of the fuel, and then basically starved the engines. It would be a pretty easy way to deliberately sabotage a plane going on a route like ours through mountains and forest terrain, with no easy place to land. And a crash would burn away all the fuel, making the tampering virtually untraceable."

Shelby leaned her head back against the tree behind her. What could she say to that? Had someone really tried to kill her *three* times in the past twenty-four hours?

"It just seems so far-fetched."

Dylan began to stand. "I know. Whatever those numbers are that are stuck in your head? Evidently they're more important than you or Megan or anybody at Omega thought. We need to get you there as soon as possible." Dylan had to grab the tree for support. Shelby scrambled to her feet to help him.

"Before we go anywhere, we need to bandage that arm. Are you hurt anywhere else?" she asked him.

"I don't think so," Dylan muttered. "It's hard to tell. Everything hurts." He looked up at her. "Are you okay? I didn't even ask."

"Well, it's like you said—everything hurts. But nothing hurts too much to move it. So that's good."

Shelby took the first-aid kit out of the backpack. She sat down next to Dylan and rolled his sleeve up. The cut on his arm was still bleeding, but not too bad. It didn't look like it would need stitches. Shelby ripped open a small package of antibiotic ointment and squeezed it over the wound to help keep any infection out. Dylan winced, but didn't complain. Shelby covered the wound, then wrapped his arm in gauze.

"Thank you," he said softly when she was finished.

"Thank you for getting us on the ground in one piece when almost any other pilot would've scattered us in little-bitty bits around the forest."

"Well, that's pretty gruesome imagery. But you're welcome."

DYLAN STOOD UP and watched his Cessna burning. He was glad he was able to get himself and Shelby on the ground relatively unharmed, and not in little-bitty bits as Shelby had pointed out so delicately.

There was an old pilot's joke that any landing you could walk away from was a landing not a crash. But watching his plane burn, Dylan knew that wasn't true. He felt a pang of sadness. Even though insurance would cover the cost of a similar new plane, it wouldn't be the same. He'd traveled a lot of miles in that little Cessna. His time in that plane had gotten him through some of the worst days of his life.

Shelby didn't say anything to him and he was grateful. There weren't any words that could be said. It was a pile of metal, for heaven's sake.

But it was also so much more than that.

Dylan appreciated it even more when Shelby slipped her hands into his. Whatever she was thinking, it was supportive and it didn't need words.

Dylan stood there a few more minutes. Nothing could be saved from the plane. It wasn't even safe to go back in to try the radio or to get their cell phones. Air Traffic Control knew their basic whereabouts, but there was no way to get any rescue vehicles up here.

According to the GPS Dylan had grabbed, they were only fifteen miles south of a small town. The town hadn't had a runway, but they would have a telephone.

Dylan couldn't ignore the fact that only Omega knew Dylan was the one transporting Shelby to Washington, DC. It was possible that the person who had run Shelby off the road both times last night had followed her from her house, but this deliberate tampering with Dylan's aircraft could really only mean one thing.

There was somebody within Omega working against them.

Dylan didn't even like to think it, but it was the only thing that made sense. Whoever had sabotaged his plane had done it last night during the storm. Dylan had flown the Cessna yesterday and there hadn't been anything wrong with it.

And over the past year, all his siblings had grumbled about the possibility of a mole in Omega. Problems here and there within operations, but never anything that could be proven. But standing here watching his plane burn, knowing neither he nor Shelby should've been alive after that crash, Dylan had all the proof he needed of a mole.

And while Dylan wouldn't directly accuse anyone without more proof, he had to admit that a lot of this was pointing right at Dennis Burgamy, his old boss. Burgamy had sent Shelby to him, had known they'd be using Dylan's plane.

That was pretty damning evidence.

"We're not going to have to walk all the way to Christiansburg, are we? That's sixty miles away, right? I heard you tell Air Traffic Control." Shelby looked up at him, brows furrowed.

Dylan put his hand against her cheek and smoothed his thumb over her brows to ease the worry lines before he even realized what he had done. He rubbed his thumb over her lip and stepped closer to her, but then stopped himself. He lowered his hand and stepped back. Touching Shelby was not a good idea.

Dylan cleared his throat. "Um, no. There's another town closer. About fifteen miles. With this terrain, it should take us five or six hours to walk. We should get started."

Dylan turned away from her, trying to remember all the reasons why he needed to keep his distance. Damned if he could think of a single one of them.

Chapter Ten

Dylan had insisted on carrying the backpack, although Shelby had offered because of his wounded arm. After touching her so gently, then completely backing away, Dylan had busied himself taking everything out of the backpack. She noticed he was quite careful not to touch her again.

The backpack was obviously his overnight bag. It contained mostly a change of clothes and some toiletry items. But he also had a can of soda, a few packs of trail mix, some bottles of water and even a couple of trash bags. Plus the lunch he had packed for himself.

"Lunch?"

"I packed it last night while you were sleeping. The airstrip we would've used for Omega only has vending machines. I thought I might be turning around to go home right away."

"Weren't you going to see your siblings while you were in town? Have lunch with them?"

Dylan shrugged, but didn't look her in the eye.

"Maybe. I wasn't sure. I didn't want to be in the way of whatever you were doing."

In other words, he would've visited with his family if it meant he wouldn't have to spend extra time with Shelby. But just in case being in Shelby's presence was unavoidable, he had packed a lunch so he could make a quick getaway in his plane.

"Nice," Shelby muttered. She wasn't sure why she was so hurt. Dylan Branson had made it abundantly clear multiple times he wanted to spend as little time with her as possible.

"Look, it's nothing personal," he told her, taking the useless items like shaving cream and toothpaste out of the backpack.

"It feels pretty personal."

Dylan looked up from where he was crouched, his hazel eyes pinning her. "Yeah, I suppose it would." He rubbed his fingers over his eyes. "There are elements to this story that you're not aware of. And I'm sorry I keep hurting your feelings, but it's just better for both of us if I stay away from you."

Shelby had no idea what she was supposed to say to that.

Not that she was going to get a chance to anyway. Dylan left the pile of items he deemed useless for their hike, repacked the helpful things—the clothes, food, drinks, trash bags—into the backpack and stood up. "We need to get going."

He turned and began walking. Shelby was left with the choice of following or being left behind. They walked in silence for a while. The terrain wasn't easy; there weren't any roads or paths this far away from civilization.

As trees and bushes got thicker, Shelby found herself walking closer to Dylan. He had wrapped his extra shirt around his good arm so he could move limbs and bushes out of their way without getting scratched. After the first time of Dylan having to wait holding a branch for Shelby to catch up, she stayed right behind him.

As they marched on, the weather became less cooperative. The temperatures were already cold and the clouds were beginning to threaten storms again. Shelby found she could keep the core of her body warm by the constant moving, but her fingers were freezing. Her feet were wet from the soggy ground and she had lost feeling in her toes an hour ago.

When it started to drizzle, Shelby just ducked her head down and pushed her chilled hands into her pockets, although it didn't help much. The cold rain occasionally dripped down her neck, but Shelby plowed on. She reminded herself that just a couple short hours ago she had been sure they were about to die. Being a little wet and uncomfortable was bearable.

But she still shuddered when another cold drop of rain found its way through the trees and down the neck of her shirt.

She forced herself to trudge on step after step, trying to think about anything but her own misery. Mostly that included trying to think of the *elements* of Dylan's story that she wasn't aware of. Although she knew she shouldn't care.

Shelby didn't realize Dylan had stopped walking and slammed right into his broad back. His reflexes were quick. He reached his good arm around his back to steady her against him.

"You okay?" he asked.

"Yeah." Cold. Tired. Hungry. Stressed. Miserable. "I'm fine."

"This storm is moving in quickly. It's only drizzling now, but soon it will be pouring. We're going to need to find somewhere to hunker down. Hypothermia can become an issue even in these temps if we let ourselves get too wet."

Shelby gritted her teeth to keep them from chattering. It was probably in the upper fifties, but she felt much colder in her shirt and lightweight jacket. "Where?" She forced the word out, sticking her numb hands under her armpits.

"We're going to build a wickiup. It won't be perfect, but it will be something." Shelby watched almost in a daze as Dylan began gathering thin branches about four to five feet in length.

"A wickiup?"

"It's also called a debris hut. It won't be fancy, but it will get us through the next few hours. We're going to build it up against that overturned tree. It'll provide us with a good deal of shelter from the rain all on its own."

Shelby looked over at the tree Dylan pointed at. She felt as if her brain was processing information too slowly. Dylan, on the other hand, was moving quickly, efficiently. Not unlike when she had watched him go through his preflight checklist. He had done this before.

He looked around for something, and then evidently found what he needed: a stick of a specific size, about six feet long, thicker than the others.

"This will be our ridgepole." He wedged one end of the stick into the overturned tree, about four feet up, and wedged the other end into a spot on the ground. "Now we add branches to make a lattice."

Slowly, Shelby's brain began to process. He was making them a shelter. It wouldn't be very big, but it would maybe keep them drier and warmer. She looked up at the clouds that were now ominous overhead.

She needed to start functioning and help. Shelby began gathering sticks similar to the size

Dylan was using to frame his construction. He seemed surprised when she handed the first few she found to him, but then nodded.

"Thanks. We'll need to hurry if we're going to beat this storm."

"How many more do you need?" she asked him.

"At least a dozen."

Shelby began to scramble for them as Dylan took some items out of the backpack. Trash bags.

"One of the disadvantages of owning your own charter business? You're also the cleanup crew. But these will come in handy keeping out the rain." He took his pocketknife and began to slice them lengthwise. "We'll use them as tarps."

The thunder boomed from the clouds overhead, causing Shelby to drop her sticks. She bent down to pick them up again and brought them over to Dylan.

"Good," he said as he stretched the trash bag over the frame he had built and pinned it to the ground. "Try to find as much dry pine straw, grass, leaves, anything we can use to put on the ground and over the tarp."

Shelby brought anything she thought might be useful. Some he used, some he didn't, but the rain was picking up, making gathering more material impossible.

Thunder boomed again and rain began to fall in earnest.

"That's it. We'll do more damage than good if we bring anything in now. It'll be too wet. Let's get in. I'll go first since it will be easier for you to work your way around me."

He wasted no time, throwing the backpack into the shelter then sliding himself headfirst into the small enclosure. There was barely room for Dylan. How was Shelby supposed to fit?

"Okay, I'm in. It's pretty cramped."

A blast of thunder eliminated any further hesitation Shelby felt. She climbed in as rain began to really pour down around her. She slid as far as she could. Dylan's arm reached around her and slid her fully inside.

The shelter was cramped, no doubt, but it was also warm and dry. Shelby took a moment to enjoy being out of the wet and wind; the tension she'd been carrying eased some. Dylan was lying flat, his head resting against the backpack. There was no room to sit or shift around.

The warmth felt delightful and Shelby felt herself relaxing. Her head slowly drooped until it came to rest on the hard ground. Except it wasn't the hard ground. It was Dylan's muscular chest. Shelby realized how much of her body was lying on Dylan's body. There really wasn't any way around it. There was no room.

But unwilling to trigger one of Dylan's cooties attack where he didn't want to touch her, Shelby tried to pull herself back and away from him. But his large body seemed to completely fill up the shelter.

"You might as well relax. We're going to be stuck here for a while. At least it's warm and dry." Dylan shifted and pulled Shelby closer, but she still resisted.

"What?" he asked her, his voice deep and soft.

Shelby sighed and closed her eyes. She could not be thinking how deep and soft his voice was. Not trapped in this little shelter with a storm raging outside.

And especially not because at any moment he might decide he couldn't stand to be near her. Again.

"I just don't want to make you uncomfortable. You seem to do okay, but then something happens and you…"

"I what?"

"I don't know. Panic or something. Like you've got to get away from me as soon as possible."

That was met with silence. Shelby didn't even know why she had brought it up. She leaned up on her elbow so she could try to see him in the mostly dark enclosure. "Look, you're not into me. I get it. It's not a prob—"

His lips stopped the flow of her words and

wrecked Shelby's train of thought. Her eyes closed as his hand reached up to wrap behind her neck and pull her down more firmly against him. He teased her lips apart slowly, nibbling at them.

All Shelby could hear was the rain and all she could feel was Dylan. And that was just fine. His other arm came up to wrap around her waist.

The kiss went on as Dylan pulled her closer, shifting her weight until she was almost fully lying on top of him. He traced her lips with his tongue and she opened her mouth, giving them both the access they wanted.

But another large crack of thunder, directly over them, startled them apart. Shelby opened her eyes to find Dylan looking at her. He stared at her for long moments.

"I'm into you. That is definitely not the problem."

But Shelby noticed he didn't pull her back in for another kiss. Not that they could do much more anyway in the middle of the wilderness in a lightning storm.

Instead, he slid her weight off him by rolling slightly to the side so she was tucked next to him. Then pulled her head down against his chest so she rested against him. Shelby gave up any thought of trying to keep distance between them. She just relaxed. His arm around her began playing with her hair.

Neither of them said anything for a long time as the storm continued to rage overhead. Shelby was amazed at how well the shelter held.

"I can't believe we're still dry. You must have made one of these shelters before." She remembered the deftness he had shown when putting it together.

"Yeah. It was part of my training in the army. We had to build field-expedient shelters—ones made out of only natural objects. You can stay relatively dry in those, but having the trash bags really helped."

"How long were you in the army?"

"Six years. Got my college degree and pilot experience while I was in, so a pretty good deal for me overall."

"And then you went to work for Omega Sector." Shelby could feel Dylan begin to tense at the mention of the law enforcement group he once worked for, but had no idea why.

"Yes. They recruited me, actually."

"Were you a pilot for them?"

"On some missions, but not necessarily. I was an undercover agent. So I used whatever I could to give me an in with certain criminals. Being a pilot helped in a lot of situations."

"Your siblings all work for Omega?" It was difficult to concentrate with Dylan making circles on her waist and hip with his hand. "They like it?"

"Yeah. Everyone has had their ups and downs, but none of them seem to want to leave."

"Why did you leave?"

Dylan's hand stopped moving then. It dropped away from her body altogether. He was silent for so long Shelby thought he was going to refuse to answer.

"An operation went wrong. And some people were hurt because I made stupid mistakes. I got out right after that."

Shelby was quiet for a moment. She could feel Dylan's heart beating in his chest that rested under her ear. She trailed her hand that rested at his waist up his torso. She sat up so she could look him in the eye. She cupped his cheek with her hand.

"I'm sure it wasn't your fault. Anybody working at Omega has to know there are risks involved."

"These were innocent people. Not agents."

Shelby knew she should just leave it alone, but somehow couldn't. "But still, you can't control everything. I'm sure it wasn't—"

"It was my wife and unborn child that died. I led a member of a crime syndicate group right to them. He shot her right in front of me before I could do anything about it."

Dylan flinched from Shelby's hand that still rested on his cheek, so she moved it. She lay back down, unable to stand the agony in Dylan's eyes any longer.

This explained so much of his hot-and-cold reactions toward her. Dylan was obviously still in love with his dead wife. Shelby knew he wished he didn't have to touch her right now, but she was unable to do anything about it in the cramped enclosure. Her head now rested on his arm rather than his chest. She stared up at the ceiling of the shelter, listening to the rain.

Dylan didn't elaborate any further. Nor did the arm that had been around her touch Shelby again. Shelby was amazed at how close they could be together, yet so, so far apart.

Chapter Eleven

Dylan never liked to talk about Fiona. She had been so young, so beautiful, so full of life.

Okay, Dylan knew that wasn't totally accurate. Really, Fiona had been a little spoiled and their marriage had been a bit rocky. But you couldn't really say those things about someone who had been struck down in the prime of her life.

Dylan didn't know if his marriage to Fiona would've worked out if she had lived. But he damn well knew he would've loved that child—his son—she had been carrying. No matter what, Dylan would've loved that child.

"She was only four months pregnant," Dylan murmured. "The baby never had a chance. Sometimes I've wondered if Fiona had been further along, if the baby possibly could've made it, even if she hadn't."

Dylan had never said those words out loud to anyone. He wasn't sure why he was saying them to Shelby now. They probably made him sound like the most insensitive jerk in the history of the world.

Dylan braced himself for whatever Shelby would say, because no matter what it was, it wouldn't be right. Nothing could be said to make the situation right.

But Shelby didn't say anything. She just reached up and grabbed the hand of his arm that was under her head. She intertwined their fingers.

And somehow that was enough. No words were needed.

Dylan thought about Shelby as the storm raged on around them. The way she had handled this whole situation had been pretty impressive. She hadn't fallen apart, not during the crash, not afterward.

She'd marched on through the wilderness at a pretty punishing speed, although Dylan knew she had to be cold. Not once complaining. For someone who spent the majority of time by herself behind a computer, the way she was holding it together in this real-life dangerous situation was impressive.

Hell, everything about her was impressive. But Dylan knew he had to leave her alone. He had nothing to offer. He didn't even have a job now, for goodness' sake, not since his Cessna lay burned a few miles away.

The storm seemed to be moving away from

them. Good, they needed to get moving. As soon as they made it into the little town, Dylan would call for a pickup. But he wouldn't be calling Omega directly, not while there was a mole. Dylan would call the people he knew he could trust: his brothers and sister. One of them would come get them and bring them to Omega.

But maybe Dylan wouldn't leave immediately. Somebody needed to stick close to Shelby and make sure she was safe. His siblings had their hands full with their own cases and duties.

But Dylan still planned to keep his hands off the tiny redhead resting beside him. Definitely no more kisses. Because he knew he wouldn't be stopping next time, whether or not they were in the middle of a lightning storm in the wilderness.

"Sounds like it's passing through," Dylan told her. "We should be able to get going again in a few more minutes."

"How much farther do we have?"

"Probably eight or nine more miles. Maybe three more hours."

He heard Shelby's sigh, the first indication of stress about the situation he'd heard from her. "You're doing great. Couldn't ask for a better hiking partner."

Shelby gave the most unfeminine grunt Dylan had ever heard. He couldn't help laughing.

Dylan released Shelby's hand and shifted

around behind him to get the backpack. "Let's eat the food. No point carrying it when we're hungry."

"Definitely."

They made short work of the sandwiches and soda from Dylan's lunch. It wasn't enough to fill them up given the number of calories they were expending, but at least it took the edge off. They decided to save the trail mix and water for later when they'd need it.

Eating lying down wasn't easy, but they managed. By the time they had finished the sandwiches, the worst of the storm had passed. The thunder and lightning were gone.

"Are you ready to get going?" he asked her. He knew neither of them were thrilled at the thought of hours of walking in the cold, but it was just going to get worse if they had to go after the sun went down. They definitely didn't want to be stranded out in the wilderness overnight if they had any other option.

"Yep." Shelby didn't sound enthused, but she certainly wasn't complaining either. A lot of other women wouldn't be so tough. Fiona sure wouldn't have been. Damn it, Dylan had to stop comparing Shelby to Fiona. Shelby seemed to win every time, which couldn't be fair, right? Fiona was dead and couldn't defend herself. Shelby was very much alive.

For some reason, a quote from the one literature class Dylan had taken in college came to mind. From Shakespeare, if he remembered correctly.

Though she be but little, she is fierce.

Yeah, that was Shelby. Fierce.

Dylan turned to her. "The walk is going to be tough, but you've been doing really well."

Shelby rolled her eyes. "Thanks. I don't necessarily feel that way, but thanks."

Dylan nodded. "We're going to try to salvage the trash bags, in case we need to reuse them. As a matter of fact, you might want to wrap one around yourself if you're getting dripped on too much."

"It's my hands that get really cold. I wish I had some gloves."

It was only the beginning of November, but in the mountains with the rain, it was easy to get chilled. Especially someone with as little insulation as Shelby.

"I have extra socks in the backpack. They aren't gloves, but they'll at least give you a little covering."

"I'll take them. Thanks."

Dylan slid out of the shelter, wincing a little at the ache in his arm. It was painful, but not unmanageable, so he put it out of his mind. The rain had mostly stopped, but he could tell the difference in temperature immediately.

Shelby slid out behind him. "Wow, we would've been in trouble without the shelter."

Dylan set down the backpack and took out the socks, handing them to Shelby. "Here, put these on."

"Let me help you take down the shelter first."

Dylan shook his head. "No, it's all wet. You need to stay as dry and warm as possible, not get wet taking this apart."

"But what about you?"

"I've got quite a bit more body mass than you. It'll take a lot more than some wet sticks to get me cold." He pointed to the socks. She was already shifting back and forth to keep warm. "Go ahead and put those on."

As she did so, Dylan grabbed the trash bag they had used on the ground, getting off as much of the leaves and debris they'd piled on it for warmth as he could. When he had shaken off as much as possible, he folded it and put it next to the backpack. Then he walked around the frame of the structure to get the other trash bag.

And nearly stepped on a large snake that was coming out from under some bushes.

Dylan immediately froze, hoping his stillness would cause the snake to just slither off in the other direction. But the snake coiled and slid its head back, ready to strike. Dylan knew by the shape of its head and coloring it was poisonous.

"Uh, whatcha doing over there, playing freeze tag?" Shelby began walking in his direction.

"No, Shelby, stay back!" Dylan's voice was barely more than a whisper, but as forceful as he could make it. If she came over here, it might cause the snake to strike.

"What is it?"

"A copperhead. Right in front of me. Ready to strike."

And the snake was angry.

Dylan knew if he got bit by a poisonous snake this far away from town, it would probably be deadly. There was no way Shelby would be able to get him all those miles by herself. And by the time she could get people back to Dylan…

A tree branch near Dylan swayed in the wind and the snake struck. Dylan jerked back, barely making it out of the snake's reach. It immediately coiled and reared its head back once more.

Snake attacks were based on movement. Dylan tried to hold as still as possible, hoping the snake would soon just go its own way. But the tree branches moving around Dylan were keeping the copperhead on high alert. And from this angle, there was no way Dylan could scoop the snake away with a stick without being bitten.

Out of the corner of his eye, Dylan saw Shelby

making her way around the far side of where the deadly pit viper was coiled.

"Shelby, what are you doing? Stop."

She totally ignored him.

"I'm not kidding, Shelby," Dylan muttered without taking his gaze from the snake in case it struck again.

"You can't get it from where you are, I can," Shelby murmured. Dylan saw the long stick in her hand.

He was about to warn her not to move any closer, when she scooped her stick under the snake and flung it—stick and all—as hard as she could away from them.

It wasn't necessarily elegant, but it got the job done. The copperhead was gone.

Shelby all but leaped at Dylan.

"It's gone, right? Please tell me it's gone and not coming back because I definitely do not have it in me to do that again. I really don't like snakes." A shudder racked her body.

"No, I'm pretty sure its twenty-foot flight through the air scared it away from here." He grabbed her shoulders to hold her still from the get-the-snake-away-from-me dance she was doing. "You shouldn't have done that. You could've been bitten."

The thought of that viper ripping into Shelby's

delicate skin was something close to horrifying to Dylan. It made him angry to even think about it.

"No offense, but you were in much more danger of that than me. Ugh." She shuddered again. "Did you see me, Dylan? I was like something out of one of my games. Maybe I should write a situation like that into one." She elbowed him in the stomach and actually laughed.

Damn it, she wasn't even taking her close call seriously. How could she be that flippant with her life? Dylan took her by the shoulders and set her abruptly away from him. "Don't do something that stupid again. Why don't you use your brain for something more than just prying into my personal business, so we can both get out of here alive?"

As soon as he said the words, Dylan wished he could take them back. Damn it, that wasn't how he felt. Shelby hadn't been prying earlier, she'd just been making conversation.

He saw her eyes widen in shock from the sucker punch he'd delivered. He had to apologize. "Shelby—"

Her eyes dropped from his, her red hair creating a veil around her face as she studied the ground with a great deal of attention. She turned and stepped away. "No, you're right. I do need to stop being so stupid."

Somehow Dylan didn't think she was referring to copperheads. "No, Shelby, please…"

Dylan trailed off as she continued to step back from him, still looking down at the ground. "Like you said, we need to get going. I'll be more careful."

Dylan couldn't let this stay between them. He moved to stand right in front of her and reached over with both hands to tuck her hair behind her ears so he could see her face, then tilted her head back. Her eyes met his for just a moment then looked away.

"I'm sorry. What I said was unfair and untrue. You haven't pried at all. You…" *Distract me. Have my attention all the time. Make me forget that I'm no good for a long-term relationship. You make me want to kiss you just by standing there breathing.* "You scared me with that snake and I was stupid. I'm sorry."

She still wasn't really looking at him. Dylan took a half step closer so their faces were only inches apart. Then Shelby didn't have any choice but to look at him.

"I'm a pretty solitary guy, Shelby. I'm not around people too often and around gorgeous women like you even less. But that's no excuse for what I said. I'm sorry."

Shelby nodded slightly. "Okay."

Dylan stepped back. Or, he meant to step back, planned to step back. But instead, he brought his lips down to Shelby's and kissed her. Softly. With reverence.

An apology.

Although she didn't pull away, Shelby's lips were closed and unmoving under his. Dylan knew he should stop, should just end the kiss and let it go, but somehow he couldn't. He couldn't let her stay distant from him. He continued his gentle onslaught of her lips. Eventually Shelby sighed and leaned in closer, returning his kiss. Her arms traveled up his arms and wound around his neck.

A few drops of cold water falling from the trees above them reminded Dylan that they needed to get moving. He pulled back from Shelby, resting his forehead against hers.

"I guess we should get going," she whispered, her voice husky.

"Yeah. We don't want to get caught out here once it's dark."

They worked together to take down the other tarp and fold it up. They took a few sips of water and were on their way.

And although Shelby didn't seem to be hurt or angry anymore, there seemed to be a definite distance between them, despite their kiss.

Dylan knew that should be what he wanted.

He knew her emotional distance shouldn't bother him. But it did.

More than he was willing to admit.

Chapter Twelve

Five hours later they made it into the small town they'd been aiming for. Pulaski, Virginia. Dylan had to admit, he was relieved. Although he was pretty adept with a geospatial map and compass, both of which he'd had in the backpack, even the best navigator could have problems in the weather and circumstances he and Shelby had been through.

The town was even smaller than Falls Run, and when Dylan and Shelby stumbled into the first building they came to—a small hardware store—they found they were already celebrities.

They were barely inside the door when a teenager working there squealed, "Oh, my gosh, you guys are the ones from the plane crash, right? You're alive. Oh, my gosh."

Dylan looked at Shelby, confusion mirroring on both of their faces.

He turned back to the girl, who was now getting her smartphone out to take pictures. "I'm sorry, how do you know we crashed our plane?"

"Are you kidding? *Everybody* knows. County emergency services came through this morning making an announcement that they'd been notified about an emergency landing of a plane somewhere nearby. Nobody knew exactly where."

"Wow," Shelby murmured.

The teenager didn't stop talking. "A couple groups of locals went out looking for you in the general direction emergency services thought you'd be, but they weren't sure how far to go, so I think they came back—

"Mom!" the teenager yelled in the middle of her own sentence, startling both Dylan and Shelby. "Those people from the airplane crash are here. Here in the store." Her voice dipped down to a more reasonable level. "No offense, but you guys look a little rough. Actually, I guess you guys look pretty good for having survived a plane crash."

"We were lucky," Dylan said. But listening to the young girl talk nonstop, Dylan was beginning to rethink that sentiment. Thankfully, the mother, a much more calm lady, came out of the back room.

"Oh, my goodness. A lot of people have been looking for you two." The woman looked over at her daughter who was still taking pictures with her cell phone. "Angi, get them some water bottles from the back."

The mom brought folding chairs over for Dylan and Shelby, which they gratefully accepted.

"Are you seriously injured? Do we need to call for an ambulance? The nearest hospital is about forty miles away, but we have a doc-in-a-box closer."

"No." Dylan shook his head then took the water bottle Angi brought them from the back. "We're both pretty bruised and banged up, but nothing too serious. I just need to use a phone if that's okay."

The hardware store door chimed behind them and Dylan looked over. A number of people were coming through the door. Even more were standing outside.

The mom shrugged. "Evidently Angi has posted your miraculous survival on all her many social media sites. We don't get a lot of action in a town this small. You're a pretty big deal."

Dylan sighed. He didn't suppose much damage would come from one teenager posting their picture all over her instant-photo account, but he would've preferred not to have any record of him and Shelby here at all.

Shelby was sitting over in her seat staring blankly to the side. She was exhausted, not that Dylan could blame her. Dylan needed to call

Sawyer and Megan to get them updated on the situation, and Sawyer could get down here and pick them up. But Dylan also needed some food for Shelby and a place where she could get a little rest.

Dylan stood up and walked with the mom a few steps away. "Look, Shelby and I really appreciate how worried everyone has been about us, but we really need to get some food and lie down, not talk to a bunch of people right now. Does this town have a hotel? Somewhere we can stay until our family comes to get us?"

The mom shook her head. "No hotel, but we have a furnished studio room upstairs you can use. We rent it out to campers during the summer. It's not fancy, but it has a bed and a shower."

"That would be perfect. Thank you."

"You take care of your wife. I'll get rid of the crowd and then get you a phone to use."

Dylan didn't bother to correct her, just walked over to Shelby and crouched beside her. "You doing okay?"

Shelby nodded. "Just tired. And hungry."

"I'm going to call Sawyer and Megan, then we'll grab something to eat. While we're waiting for them to get us, the lady has offered us the room upstairs to rest, okay?"

Dylan wasn't sure exactly how much of what he was saying Shelby was processing. She'd been quiet most of the past few hours. Some of it was exhaustion, but some of it was her keeping her distance from him.

Mrs. Morgan, the mom, shooed all the people away, knowing most of them by name. Someone said they would inform the county emergency services that Dylan and Shelby were alive. Everyone was excited. Dylan heard the word *miracle* muttered more than once.

"I'm going to go get you two some food," Mrs. Morgan came back to tell them after she'd gotten all the townspeople out of her store. "If you try to go out there now, I'm afraid you'll be mobbed. A friendly mob, but mob nonetheless."

"Thank you, Mrs. Morgan. We appreciate that," Shelby told the older woman.

Interesting that Shelby seemed to have enough energy to talk to everyone but Dylan. He could feel his face tighten.

"Here's the phone you wanted, honey." Mrs. Morgan handed Dylan a smartphone bedazzled with all shades of turquoise. "It's Angi's. Why don't you go back in the storage room if you need some quiet to talk."

Dylan knew he wouldn't have to worry about not being able to see in the closet because of all the multiple jewels shining on the phone.

He dialed Sawyer's personal phone number.

"Yes? This is Sawyer Branson." Dylan knew his brother didn't recognize the number.

"Hey, bro."

Dylan could hear Sawyer's sigh of relief. "Thank God."

"Are you where you can talk?" Dylan asked him.

"I'm at work."

"It's looking like that's not a place where you can talk." Dylan didn't want to make any accusations or suggestions while someone at Omega might overhear their conversation.

"Can I call you back at this number in five minutes? It won't be from my regular number. I'll be using a burner phone." Sawyer had learned how a known cell phone could be used against him on a case not too long ago.

Dylan waited for Sawyer's return call, amazed by the number of push notifications Angi got on her phone. Evidently she was the town's superstar since she had posted pictures of Dylan and Shelby on every social media site available. She'd even selfied herself into one of them, getting Dylan and Shelby in the background. Dylan rolled his eyes.

Ten more notifications came in before Sawyer's call came in a minute later.

"Okay, I'm out of Omega," Sawyer told him. Dylan could vaguely hear the sound of downtown

DC traffic around Sawyer. "I texted Megan to meet me out here. She's been worried sick."

"So you know about the plane crash?"

"When you didn't show up at the scheduled time, we started checking for problems with Air Traffic Control. Your Mayday was at the top of their list. What the hell happened?"

Dylan rubbed a tired hand over his eyes. "We were sabotaged, Sawyer. Someone was deliberately trying to take us down and make it look like an accident."

Sawyer's muttered curse was foul. "How?" he asked after a moment.

Dylan appreciated that his brother didn't question his assessment of the situation. "If I had to guess, some sort of fuel contaminant. Something I wouldn't notice during preflight, but was sure to cause huge problems while in the air. Both engines flamed out."

Another string of obscenities were cut off midstream. "Hang on, Megan just got here."

Dylan could hear Sawyer tell Megan that he and Shelby were okay. He could hear Megan's relieved cries. And then she was on the phone.

"Dylan, you guys are really okay? Shelby, too?"

"Yes, I promise, Megan. A few cuts, shaken up, yes. And some smoke inhalation. But overall, we're in good shape. Shelby's getting something to eat right now."

"Okay. I'll let you talk to Sawyer again. We need to get you guys here quickly. See you soon, Dyl."

"Shelby will be glad to see you, Megan," Dylan told her softly. That set Megan off on a new round of tears.

"My hormonal, pregnant wife is now sobbing," Sawyer said.

"I'm sorry, Sawyer." Dylan hadn't meant to cause Megan undue stress.

"Don't worry about it. She cried this hard a couple of days ago because she saw a double rainbow."

Dylan could hear Sawyer's "ouch" as Megan evidently did him some sort of bodily harm at his comment.

"We need a pickup." Dylan gave Sawyer the name and location of the town. "And, Sawyer, this needs to be kept on the DL. Sabotage of my plane meant that someone knew *I* was delivering Megan. That info could've only come from Omega."

"Yeah, that thought already occurred to me."

"Shelby had already had two attempts on her life before we even got into the plane."

"Are you serious? Was she involved in the motel fire last night?"

That was news to Dylan. "What motel fire?"

"The motel in Falls Run. A fire burned half the

building to the ground. There were no reports of injuries, so I figured Shelby hadn't stayed there."

Dylan cursed. "She would've been there. I got her out because I knew it would be too easy to find her there."

And a good thing Dylan had. Whoever had almost hit Shelby in the sedan obviously had come back to finish the job. If she had stayed at the hotel, she would've been an easy target. The killer could've either broken into the room or flushed her out with the fire and taken her out then. Could've easily made it look like an accident.

"Damn, Dylan," Sawyer said.

"Somebody has a real jonesing for getting rid of Shelby, that's for sure. Whatever codes are in her head must be pretty important."

"Agreed. And if it's someone at Omega who wants her dead, that's even more of a problem." Sawyer's voice was tight. Dylan knew his brother understood the gravity of the situation.

"I'm afraid it's coming from pretty high up, Sawyer."

"How high?"

"I just find it very interesting that Burgamy called me himself to set up this whole transfer. He definitely knew where Shelby would be and that we'd be on that plane."

Sawyer whistled through his teeth. "That would

explain a lot of mishaps we've had in the past on different operations."

"I know. We've got to keep our location out of Burgamy's reach."

"Agreed. I'll work on the best way to come and get you that's completely under the radar. That'll probably be by car. So plan to see us in about four hours."

"Sounds good, we could use a little downtime until then. I'm not sure if I'll have this phone with me. But the owner can get me the message. We're at the only hardware shop here in town."

"Got it. Get some rest, bro," Sawyer said.

"Yeah."

"And, Dylan, we're glad you're all right. When they told us about your Mayday, I knew if I had to be going down in a plane, you would be my best chance of surviving."

"Thanks, man."

They disconnected the call. Dylan let out a quiet exhale. Knowing his brother was on the way took some of the pressure off, especially since Sawyer was circumventing normal Omega channels.

Dylan exited the storage room and found Shelby eating with Mrs. Morgan and Angi at a little table in the main room. Shelby seemed to be doing better, and although she wasn't saying much, was smiling at whatever stories the other two women were telling.

She looked over in Dylan's direction. Her eyes met his for just a moment before dropping away. Her smile faded completely.

"Finished your call?" Mrs. Morgan asked him. "We've got food here for you."

Dylan joined them and ate, and although Mrs. Morgan and Angi had plenty to ask him and talk about, Shelby had withdrawn. She didn't talk to him, barely looked at him.

Dylan realized she was emotionally removing herself from him and the situation. He couldn't really blame her after the way he'd run so hot and cold with her.

But Dylan knew, as he sat eating his fried chicken, looking at the woman who was looking everywhere else but at him, that he wasn't going to let her withdraw.

He couldn't.

Chapter Thirteen

Dylan was looking at her.

Of course, obviously he was looking at her because they were the only two people in the studio
apartment that the friendly Mrs. Morgan and her
slightly bratty daughter, Angi, had shown them
to above the hardware store.

But he was *looking* at her. The way a man looks
at a woman when he has something planned. That
involved a bed.

And it was interesting Dylan was looking at her
now, because Shelby had pretty much decided she
wasn't going to look at Dylan anymore.

Because she'd only known him twenty-four
hours and he had already ripped her heart out
more times than most anyone else she knew. Not
that she tended to let anyone close enough to do
that, but she had been unable to help it in this
situation.

Shelby understood Dylan's hot-and-cold behavior, she really did. His wife and unborn child

dying right in front of him? That had to mess somebody up pretty badly. He still loved his wife. Shelby could certainly understand that.

But she couldn't keep allowing herself to get blindsided by Dylan each time he realized he was acting on his attraction to Shelby. And Shelby knew he was attracted to her. But she also knew he didn't like it.

So the best thing Shelby could do was just keep her distance from him.

But he had to stop *looking* at her. Or else there would be no way she could do that.

Thankfully, Dylan turned away so he could lock the door that opened to the outside stairway that led down to the hardware store. Immediately he pulled the drapes all the way closed. Then turned to scope out the room, so Shelby did the same.

A king-size bed dominated most of it. Shelby stood staring at it.

"Much better than outside in the cold, right?" Dylan asked her. "Maybe we can get a nap."

She nodded, avoiding his gaze. "For sure. How long before someone is here to pick us up?"

"Sawyer's coming, but he needs to drive, so probably about four hours."

"What do you mean he needs to drive?"

"Normally for this distance he'd take one of the

helicopters available through Omega. That would save a few hours."

"But he's not taking a helicopter now." Shelby wasn't unhappy about staying on the ground, but she didn't understand why Sawyer would delay their arrival.

Dylan looked as if he was going to say something then stopped.

"What?" she asked him. "Don't start keeping things from me now."

Dylan sighed. "When someone tried to kill you yesterday, that could've come from multiple sources. Somebody following you from your house, or perhaps an intercepted transmission or call between you and Megan."

"Yeah, that would make sense."

"But once it became clear someone had sabotaged *my* airplane, I realized that only someone from Omega Sector could've known you'd be with me. We were definitely not followed back to my house from town yesterday evening."

All Shelby could remember about the drive back to Dylan's house was seeing her red-and-black thong hooked on his big finger. Everything after that was a mortified blur. But if he said nobody followed them, she believed him.

"So it's somebody in Omega who is trying to kill me." The very agency Megan worked for, the same agency that was supposed to be protecting her and stopping DS-13.

"It looks that way. I'm sorry, Shelby."

Shelby sat on the edge of the bed. "I wish we didn't have to go to Omega at all if there is someone there trying to kill me. Someone who obviously doesn't care if they take you down with me."

"We have to. The hardware Megan needs to use with the numbers in your head is at Omega, so Sawyer must have a plan to sneak you in. He's getting here without Omega knowing."

"Yeah, I know." Shelby heard the hesitancy in her own tone, but couldn't help it.

Dylan came to sit beside her. "Thank you for not giving up. Most people who had survived three and a half attempts on their lives, not to mention hiking a marathon through the woods, might be ready to throw in the towel."

"Three and a half attempts?"

Dylan winked at her. "Well, I figured that copperhead should at least get half credit."

And there was *the look* again. Coupled with the dimple from his smile? How in the world was Shelby supposed to resist that? She had to get out. Right now.

"Okay, well, I'm just going to take a shower." Shelby stood up abruptly and made her way into the bathroom. She saw Dylan's eyes narrow momentarily, but she didn't stop. She couldn't stay there on the bed looking at his gorgeous face.

She wasn't trying to be rude, she just needed some distance.

DYLAN WATCHED SHELBY all but run into the bathroom. He shrugged off his jacket, easing his wounded arm through the sleeve. Shelby had done a good job wrapping it. He'd planned to let the Omega doctor look at it, but that was out of the question now. It wasn't too bad. A full first-aid kit would probably be enough in the hands of any of his siblings who were trained as field medics.

But more important, Dylan didn't like the way Shelby was avoiding him. Maybe not physically—it was impossible for two people in their situation to avoid each other physically, although she was trying her best—but she was definitely closing down on him emotionally.

He'd started the emotional pull away first, so he couldn't blame Shelby. It was his own fault. It had been his MO for the past six years to keep himself separated from people, especially women.

And double especially for women who had insinuated their way under his skin in twenty-four short hours with their bravery, intelligence and beauty.

Damn it.

But those kisses today.

His body began to react just thinking about it. Those kisses had set them both on fire and it had been all Dylan could do not to make love to her right there in the middle of the wilderness only a few miles from where they'd almost died.

Dylan was a man known for his control. He liked to have control in all aspects of his world, and worked very hard to make sure he had it.

But a kiss with one small redhead had blown his control all to hell. Dylan would've made love to her in that tiny shelter, on the hard cold ground, if the thunder hadn't boomed and reminded him that they were in a pretty dangerous situation.

But now here they were: safe, warm, dry. And Shelby wouldn't look him in the eye. For the past six hours—since his asinine statement about staying out of his business—she had hardly spoken to him at all. Yesterday, Dylan might have welcomed the relief from her acerbic wit. But now he could see her withdrawal, could feel it. And it made him mad. Mostly at himself.

But Dylan would be damned if he was going to let Shelby shy away from him. He wanted her more than he'd ever wanted any other woman. Watching her in the forest had sealed it for Dylan. She had shown strength and courage under demanding circumstances that could've rightfully caused her to crumble. Would've caused *most* people to crumble.

But she hadn't crumbled. The opposite, in fact. And if it hadn't been for her quick thinking, Dylan would probably be dying of a copperhead bite right now.

Everything about her was attractive to him. And he hadn't even begun thinking about her freckles yet.

So this can't-look-you-in-the-eyes stuff was not going to cut it. If he wasn't going to withdraw, he wasn't going to let her do it either.

A few minutes later the bathroom door opened and Shelby stepped out, steam swirling around her. She was dressed in only a towel. She moved to the side, holding the towel with one hand and gesturing to the bathroom door with the other.

"All yours. I washed out my clothes, so they're still wet, but I got them out of the way enough, I think." Her smile was forced, and she was obviously uncomfortable in her state of undress.

Dylan stood up from the bed and walked slowly over to Shelby, stopping just in front of her. She was looking toward him, but still not looking *at* him.

"Shelby."

"Yes?"

"Look at me." He took a step closer to her, but she didn't look. He tipped a finger under her chin. "Look at me."

There were those gorgeous green eyes. Finally. "You're avoiding me," he whispered.

"How can I avoid you?"

"You know what I mean."

Shelby finally nodded. "I can't keep getting hurt by you, Dylan. Terrible things happened, I know, so you do whatever you have to, to protect yourself. Your defenses."

She was right. It was amazing that someone who had known him such a short time could understand so much about him. "Yes, but—"

"It's okay to have defenses, Dylan," Shelby continued. "I usually have them, too, with almost everybody. But for some reason my normal defense mechanisms don't kick in around you."

Something in Dylan eased. He knew it was selfish, but he didn't want her defenses to work around him. He wanted her to be open to him. "Shelby—"

"But you hurt me, Dylan. You keep hurting me. Because what you think you want and what you really want are two different things."

"I want you," he whispered, backing her up against the wall. "*You* are what I think I want and what I really want."

"But you might change your mind." Shelby began to look away again.

"I am not going to change my mind." Dylan brought his hands up on either side of her head, burrowing his fingers in her damp hair. "I hurt you because I'm so used to pushing everyone away, and I'm sorry. You are what I want."

He bent slightly so they were eye to eye. "I won't hurt you again."

Dylan could see the doubt in Shelby's eyes, and it killed him. He was afraid she would pull away. But she leaned toward him, putting her lips gently against his.

He was humbled by her trust in him, and kissed her back gently. But then the hunger—the *heat*—that had sparked between them since the first moment they'd met flared again. And all thought of soft and gentle was left behind.

Dylan kissed her. Kissed her in a way that left no doubt that, no matter what, they would be finishing what they started this time.

Her arms reached up to wrap around his shoulders, but Dylan grabbed her wrists and brought both arms up over her head, never stopping the kiss. He heard her soft sigh as his hands slid up from her wrists to link their fingers together.

Her mouth opened, giving him fuller access, and he took full advantage, using his tongue to duel with hers. His body, pressed up against hers, was the only thing holding her towel in place. Dylan nipped gently at her bottom lip then let go of her lips altogether, but not of her hands, which he still held over her head against the wall. He waited for her eyes to flutter open, then deliberately took a small step back.

Her towel slid down her body and pooled on the floor.

Their eyes met, then Dylan brought his lips back down to hers. He released her hands and slid his fingers into her hair and cupped the nape of her neck, drawing her even closer. Her fingers slid under his shirt, pushing it up. Dylan released her lips to tear his shirt over his head, then found her mouth again. This time he was the one moaning.

He reached down and swung her up in his arms. He walked over to the bed and laid her on it almost reverently.

Yes, she was very definitely what he wanted and he proceeded to prove it to her.

Chapter Fourteen

Shelby felt as though she'd been almost run over, had survived a plane crash and had hiked through miles of wilderness over the past twenty-four hours.

Oh, wait, she had.

To say nothing of the most incredible sex ever. That had probably come the closest to killing her. In the best way possible.

She had been determined to hold herself aloof from Dylan, especially after what he had said in the forest. He'd apologized, and they'd even kissed again, but Shelby had already emotionally withdrawn. She had just wanted to get out of the woods, get to Megan and help however she was needed, and then get away from Dylan.

But there had been no reason to sit around talking about her hurt feelings with Dylan in the forest, so Shelby had just bucked up and started walking.

Because if there was one thing Shelby's mother

had taught her, it was to buck up and move on. Shelby had never been able to please her mother. Had never been outgoing and pleasant enough; had always been too rough around the edges. Eventually Shelby had just stopped trying to please someone who couldn't accept her the way she was. It had been a long and painful lesson that had taken up most of her childhood.

But Shelby knew how to hold her head up and keep moving forward even when a little piece of her heart had cracked. And she'd done it today with Dylan.

He still loved his dead wife. Shelby understood that, couldn't even fault him for it. His coldness was understandable. But when they'd made it into town, Shelby found that she couldn't look him in the eye. That somehow, her ability to buck up and move on had failed her.

He didn't want her. And that hurt.

She'd fled to the shower where she'd been able to pull herself together. All she needed to do was make it through the next few hours until they got to Omega. Then she could say goodbye to Dylan, get the codes to Megan and her supercomputer and get back to her house in Knoxville. And maybe never leave it again.

But then she'd walked out of that shower.

She had no idea what had happened to Dylan while she was in there. Yeah, he'd been giving her *the look* before she went in. But by the time she came out of the shower, he'd been determined to get what he wanted.

And what he wanted was her.

She lay on his chest now, his fingers trailing up and down her spine.

"Your freckles drove me crazy from the first second I saw you, you know," he said against her forehead. "You're lucky you made it out of the diner without me throwing you down on the booth."

Shelby kissed his chest and laughed. "I'm pretty sure Sally would not have approved."

"And poor Tucker definitely would've had a heart attack."

Shelby felt so close to Dylan now, not just because of the incredible lovemaking, but because he was more relaxed, at ease. After everything that had happened over the past day, lying here, just enjoying Dylan's arms around her, was all Shelby wanted.

But the other part of her was waiting for Dylan to realize what he'd done, which was, in essence, to cheat on his dead wife. She was sure it wouldn't be long before the freak-out happened. Before he pushed Shelby away again, found a reason to put distance between them. That was just a matter of time, she was sure.

Their lovemaking was probably just a one-time thing. They were two people attracted to each other, but their attraction had been pushed along at breakneck speed by everything they'd been through.

Trauma-induced sex. Was that a real thing? Shelby would have to look it up. It felt as if it should be a real thing even if it wasn't currently.

Shelby wished she had her smartphone. Or was at home with her computer. Or was at home at all, where she could fall apart alone.

Oh, hell, was she about to start crying?

"You doing okay over there?" Dylan asked.

"Just feeling a little overwhelmed by everything that's happened." Shelby could feel her voice shaking. She definitely didn't want to mention that a huge part of the emotional roller coaster she was on was fear of what Dylan was going to do in the next few minutes.

But Dylan rolled to his side so he was facing her, then slid both arms around her so he could roll onto his back, bringing Shelby's entire body on top of him.

"It's okay to be overwhelmed. You've held it together for much longer than I thought you would, much longer than anyone could've expected."

Shelby nodded, feeling the bubble of panic inside her begin to lessen. "Thanks. I'm just tired." She laid her head down on his chest.

"We probably should've used our free time to rest. Not…other stuff."

Oh, no, here it came. Dylan's withdrawal. His regret about their lovemaking disguised as worry about exhaustion. Shelby tried—and failed—to keep tension from coursing through her body at Dylan's silence after his statement.

So she totally wasn't expecting him to roll himself quickly over on the bed and take her with him. She let out a small shriek before she could stop herself. Dylan reached down and hooked one of her legs up over his hips. He held most of his weight on his elbows, gazing down at her, his fingers brushing her hair away from her face on both sides.

"Of course, there was no way I was going to nap when having you naked in this bed was an option. I didn't care how exhausted I was."

Shelby felt the tension ease out of her. It was hard to be tense when someone as gorgeous as Dylan was lying naked on top of you and *obviously* wanted you.

Yeah, he might freak out, but she'd deal with that later.

Shelby wrapped the crook of her elbow around Dylan's head and pulled him down to her. She playfully grabbed his bottom lip with her teeth then let it go. "We can sleep later."

Dylan smiled, wickedness gleaming in his eyes. "Yes. Much, much later."

SHELBY WAS ASLEEP. Dylan could tell by the snores coming out of her tiny body, which were both hilarious and the most endearing thing in the history of the world. She wasn't touching Dylan at all now. Although he'd pulled her against him to hold her after their second round of absolutely fantastic sex, once she'd fallen asleep, she had immediately pulled away and rolled over to her side. Now she was curled up in a little ball.

She was used to sleeping alone. So was Dylan. It was a fitting metaphor for both of them.

Dylan didn't want to think too carefully about what had just happened. Or how unbelievably great it had been. Or how all he wanted to do was get back in bed with Shelby and wrap his body around her little, balled up body. And teach them both how to sleep with someone else.

Or maybe show her all the reasons again why they should not sleep at all.

Dylan pulled a blanket up over Shelby before he let those thoughts gain any more traction. She needed rest.

Dylan took a shower and, unlike Shelby, he at least had a fresh pair of clothes to put on. Shelby's were still wet, hanging on the sink. They wouldn't be very comfortable to put back on when Sawyer got here in a couple hours. Maybe Mrs. Morgan had or knew of a washer and dryer nearby where Dylan could at least get Shelby's clothes dried so she wouldn't have to ride for hours in a car in damp clothes.

Dylan wrote a short note for Shelby in case she woke up and laid it on his pillow. He didn't want her thinking he'd just skipped out on her.

With Shelby's wet clothes in hand, including, Lord have mercy, that red-and-black thong—he was going to get her to model that for him very soon—Dylan made his way out the door. He locked it behind him using the key Mrs. Morgan had given them and headed down the outdoor stairs.

Darkness was approaching and the small town had shut down for the day. Dylan peeked into the front of the hardware store, but didn't see either Mrs. Morgan or Angi. Perhaps they'd gone home for the day. Dylan was a little surprised neither had come to check on him and Shelby before heading out.

As Dylan turned away from the glass, something caught his attention from inside. Just a slight movement of shadow within the already dark store. Someone was in there.

Dylan moved away from the window and began walking away casually. Maybe it was Mrs. Morgan or Angi in there in the dark, although he doubted it was Angi because Dylan would've been able to see that bedazzled phone. But it just struck him as suspicious that neither of the outgoing females would not come open the front door for him.

Dylan realized he'd been through a lot over the past twenty-four hours, and maybe was overtired and hypersensitive, but his instincts were telling him something wasn't right here. His instincts had served him well over the years and he wasn't going to start ignoring them now.

Dylan continued to walk away casually, hoping whoever was in the store would think he was just some local who'd been a little nosy. But as soon as he was around the corner and out of sight, he sprinted toward the back of the building. There had to be some other door.

Dylan found the emergency-exit door completely unlocked. He wished he had a weapon besides his pocketknife as he opened the door slowly, trying to keep it from creaking. He didn't see or hear anything inside, but that didn't necessarily mean that the building was empty. Dylan kept to the shadows, allowing his eyes time to completely adjust. He edged his way along the back wall waiting for any glimpse of the shadow he'd seen moving earlier.

Nothing.

After a couple of minutes, Dylan had convinced

himself he must have been mistaken. Or if there had been someone moving around in here, that person was gone now. The emergency-exit door being open was a little suspicious, but this was a small town. People were sometimes different in a small town than a big city. More trusting.

Dylan was turning to leave when he heard it. A sort of muffled thump from the storage room where Dylan had made his call to Sawyer earlier.

Dylan grabbed a hammer—any weapon was better than none at all—and rushed to the storage room. He opened it, ready to pounce.

But there on the ground were Mrs. Morgan and Angi, both bound and gagged.

Dylan rushed to Mrs. Morgan's side and slid the gag out of her mouth. She was bleeding from where someone had hit her in the face.

"I'm so sorry," she told Dylan. "He came in with a gun, demanding to know where you were. I didn't want to tell him, but he threatened Angi. He just left." Mrs. Morgan was sobbing.

Dylan didn't wait around to reassure Mrs. Morgan that she'd done the right thing. He whipped out his pocketknife and cut through the plastic zip ties the perp had used to tie her with and ran out the door.

Mrs. Morgan could now get Angi out. But the shadow Dylan had seen a few minutes before now knew where Shelby was.

Dylan went out the front door of the store that was closer to the outdoor staircase leading up to the studio apartment. He got to the corner and stopped, whipping his head around it to look and then back. No one was on the stairs. The man was already inside.

Dylan took the stairs two at a time, praying he wasn't too late.

Chapter Fifteen

Shelby woke up out of a sound sleep as a hand covered her mouth roughly. The room was dark and she couldn't tell who was looming over her, but she knew whoever it was, it wasn't someone friendly. She jerked away and began thrashing her body, not even caring that she was completely naked.

The man's other hand grabbed her by the hair and jerked her up to a sitting position.

"Where are the codes?" The voice was pure menace in her ear. Now that he was close, she could see he was wearing something over his face so she couldn't clearly identify his features. That made him even more frightening.

Shelby shook her head since he was covering her mouth and she couldn't talk. He yanked hard on her hair again. "Where are the codes? Are they in this room or were they destroyed in the plane?"

The man removed his hand just the slightest bit so Shelby could speak, but kept a grip on her hair. She didn't know what to say. Evidently he didn't know the codes were inside Shelby's head, not on some drive somewhere.

"I don't know wh—"

The man backhanded her. Shelby could taste blood in her mouth where her teeth cut into her cheek. Her whole face felt as if it was on fire.

"You will tell me right now or I will kill you."

Shelby knew he was going to kill her either way. Where was Dylan? He'd been beside her when she fell asleep. Dread flooded her. Was Dylan already dead?

The man yanked her hair again, this time dragging her to the floor. "Where are the codes?" he snarled. He reared back and kicked her with a booted foot in her thigh and Shelby let out a scream as pain ratcheted through her.

Shelby curled into herself as the man bent down and grabbed her hair again. "No screaming. Where are the codes?" He slammed her head against the floor. Shelby fought to hold on to consciousness.

"In the bathroom!" she choked out. It was all Shelby could think of to say through the pain. "On a hard drive on the sink."

Shelby had hoped the man would go check by himself and give her a few seconds to try to get out. She knew she'd have to run outside naked, but didn't care. Naked was better than dead.

But instead, the man grabbed her by the hair again and began dragging her with him toward the bathroom. Shelby could hardly get her hurt leg under her, so he was mostly dragging her along the ground. It wouldn't take him long to figure out she'd made up the stuff about a drive being in there.

And then he was going to kill her.

She was trying to think of any possible way out of this when the door leading from the outside of the room crashed open. From where Shelby laid mostly sprawled on the floor, she watched as Dylan ran inside. A second later, a hammer flew from Dylan's hand hitting Shelby's attacker in the shoulder. He howled in pain and let go of her.

Dylan wasted no time and leaped through the room, landing on her attacker with a flying tackle. Shelby scooted as far out of the way as she could. She knew the best way she could help Dylan was to just stay out of the way.

It took all of two seconds to realize how skilled Dylan was at fighting. He'd obviously been trained in hand-to-hand combat. He did some sort of spinning-kick thing that knocked the intruder to the floor.

But the intruder was also trained at fighting. He immediately jumped up and threw quick punches and kicks at Dylan's head and torso. Some Dylan was able to block, sheltering his injured arm as much as possible, but a couple of hits he took square on the jaw.

The blows didn't even seem to slow Dylan down. It wasn't long before it became obvious that Dylan would win this fight. The other man may have been bigger, but he wasn't as quick or as smart in his moves. Dylan gave one more good punch and the intruder flew through the air and landed in an unconscious heap on the floor near the bed.

Shelby watched it all from the corner she'd backed herself into. Everything in her entire body hurt. She couldn't imagine what Dylan felt like after that fight. And she hoped that bastard lying on the floor would be in agony once he regained consciousness.

Shelby heard the distinct sound of a shotgun being cocked from the doorway. It was Mrs. Morgan.

"You two okay?" she asked, obviously ready to take down the intruder if necessary.

Dylan quickly grabbed the sheet from the bed and handed it to Shelby. She gratefully wrapped it around herself. The teenager Angi was once again taking pictures, now of the unconscious intruder. Dylan ripped the mesh material off the man's face. Shelby didn't recognize him at all, Dylan didn't seem to either.

"Mrs. Morgan, we need some of those plastic

ties that this guy used to restrain you and Angi. I need them now before he wakes."

"Angi, go get them," Mrs. Morgan told her daughter.

"But, Mom…" Angi was obviously more interested in collecting photos to post online.

"Right this second, Angi. Or I will take that phone away until you graduate."

Angi muttered under her breath about having the worst life ever, but took off.

"What exactly is going on here, Dylan?" Mrs. Morgan asked.

"The less you know about it, the better. Just know that I'm trying to get Shelby to Washington, DC, so she can help law enforcement with something very important."

"And that guy wanted to stop that from happening?" She pointed at the man on the floor.

"Yes," Dylan explained, coming over to crouch down by Shelby. He tucked a strand of hair behind her ear. "Do you need a doctor?" he whispered.

"I don't think so." Shelby's voice was hoarse even to her own ears. "My leg is hurt, but I don't think it's broken."

Dylan nodded, then reached down and kissed her forehead. Angi showed back up with plastic zip ties and Dylan secured the man's hands behind his back.

"Mrs. Morgan, I have someone from the agency

Shelby and I need to get to on his way right now to pick us up. He should be here within the hour. But can you please call your local sheriff to come arrest this guy. He's definitely going to need to be taken in."

DYLAN'S HEART BROKE every time he looked over at Shelby huddled in the corner. She was hurt, bleeding and although she had insisted she didn't need a doctor, Dylan just wanted to get everyone out of there so he could talk to her.

Actually, what he really wanted was to take her somewhere far away from here and all the people trying to kill her, and keep her safe.

And naked in bed with him. He could do both at the same time.

"Mrs. Morgan, can you please go get some ice for Shelby's face? Also, down in the storage room, I dropped her clothes. They were wet and I wanted to see if there was anywhere I could dry them."

Angi, who had miraculously stopped taking pictures with her smartphone, looked over at her mother. "She's about my size, Mom. I can find her something to wear."

Both women nodded and left to get the needed items.

The man on the floor was beginning to groan, regaining consciousness. Dylan didn't want to deal with him yet. He grabbed the man by the collar of his shirt, lifted him a few inches and then coldcocked him. The man slumped back to the ground, completely unconscious again.

Dylan looked over at Shelby's bruised, swollen face and had zero remorse about hitting a barely conscious man. He rushed over and sat down, putting his arms around her and scooping her, bedsheet and all, into his lap.

"I thought he was going to kill me, Dylan. The only reason he didn't was because he thought the codes were on a hard drive somewhere, not in my head. He wanted to know if they had been destroyed in the crash." Shelby's words were partially muffled against his chest.

"If you had told him they'd been destroyed in the crash, he probably would've killed you immediately."

"I told him they were in the bathroom."

The image of Shelby being dragged across the floor, obviously injured, would haunt Dylan forever. If he'd been just a couple minutes later, she would've been in much worse shape or possibly dead. He pulled her closer to him and kissed the top of her head.

"Are you sure you don't need a doctor?"

"He kicked my leg pretty hard. I thought it might be broken, but I don't think so."

"Let me see it."

Dylan helped her stand up then crouched back down so he could see the outer part of her thigh when she lifted the sheet. An ugly purple bruise was already beginning to form. Careful not to touch the bruised area, Dylan pressed on the other side of her leg, up and down along the bone. She didn't have any sharp pain, which probably meant no broken bone.

"I don't think it's broken, but it's probably going to hurt like hell for a while."

"Yeah, my head, too," Shelby said. "Dude thought banging it into the floor a few times would be fun."

Dylan grimaced. She might have a concussion. He brought her over to the light near the bathroom. Her pupils weren't dilated, so that was a good sign. But still, it was one more thing that was going to hurt her. He pulled her against his chest and wrapped his arms gently around her.

"Your body must be wondering if the Third World War has happened, with all the pounding it has taken over the past day and a half."

"Yeah, no kidding. But at least I'm still here."

And she wasn't even falling apart. Amazing.

Though she be but little...

The Shakespearean quote came to Dylan's mind again. Shelby was definitely fierce.

The man was beginning to groan again. Good, Dylan wanted him to wake up. He wanted to ask him a couple of questions before the sheriff came to take him.

"Stay over here," he told Shelby, helping her sit in a chair.

Dylan crossed to the man and grabbed him up off the ground and pushed him back against the bed. "Who do you work for?"

The dark-haired man looked at Dylan and shook his head, his rough features giving away nothing.

"You know the local sheriff is going to take you into custody, but it won't be long before you're transferred to Omega."

"Being in any prison would be better than what my organization would do to me because I failed."

"If they're so bad, tell me who you work for or who you work with. We can protect you."

The man smirked. "You cannot protect me. It's all you can do to protect yourself and your woman."

"How did you find us?"

"It was only a matter of listening to the transmissions of emergency services for this area. It's all they've been talking about for hours."

Dylan was about to ask more questions—although he honestly didn't expect to get any other information out of the guy—when Mrs. Morgan came back up, Angi and the sheriff in tow.

"Mr. Branson, I'm Sheriff Fossen. I understand

you had a tussle with this fellow, who also broke in downstairs and threatened and unlawfully restrained Mrs. Morgan and her daughter."

Dylan walked over to shake the sheriff's hand. Since the sheriff already had enough to arrest the man, Dylan didn't mention that the man had also assaulted Shelby. That would lead to having to stay around here for too long. They needed to be free to go when Sawyer arrived.

"Well, I'm going to put some proper cuffs on him and take him in."

"Yeah. I think there's going to be a lot of people who have questions for him," Dylan told the sheriff. He was looking over at Shelby to make sure she was all right, when he saw movement from the bed out of the corner of his eye.

Dylan immediately moved toward Shelby to protect her, but the attacker wasn't headed her way.

Instead, the man ran across the room in the other direction and hurled himself, headfirst, out the second-story window.

The sheriff already had his weapon in hand and he and Dylan rushed to the window. The man lay on the ground twenty feet below, unmoving. The unnatural angle of his neck attested to his demise.

The man had killed himself rather than be arrested and brought in for questioning. Damn it. He definitely worked for DS-13, and now they'd never know if he had been sent directly from the mole in Omega.

Dylan crossed back over to where Shelby still sat in the chair. Mrs. Morgan was yelling at Angi not to take pictures of the dead man out the window. Sheriff Fossen was calling in what had happened on his radio and making his way out the door and down the stairs.

Dylan grabbed the clothes Angi had brought for Shelby from on top of the dresser by the door. He was just helping her stand and make her way into the bathroom so she could change when he heard his brother Sawyer from the door.

"Looks like I missed quite a party."

Chapter Sixteen

Dylan had never felt so relieved to see someone in his entire life. He walked over to hug his brother. "I'm glad you're here, man."

"What the hell happened, Dylan? Some sheriff guy just flew down those stairs like he'd heard the donut shop was about to close or something."

"Somebody attacked Shelby, was going to kill her."

They both looked over at Shelby who was still standing outside the bathroom door, wrapped in her sheet, staring at them. Sawyer walked around Dylan and sauntered over to stand right in front of her. Dylan watched as his baby brother, the flirt of the family, wrapped his arms around Shelby, picked her all the way off her feet and kissed her smack on the mouth.

Sawyer had been kissing girls on the mouth since he was three years old. And as he'd gotten older, he'd continued to love them, and kiss them. Sawyer had kissed all his brothers' girlfriends in that friendly manner. Hell, Sawyer had even kissed Fiona on the lips the day Dylan and Fiona got married.

Sawyer's kisses had never bothered Dylan before. But the sight of his brother's lips on Shelby's triggered an ugly jealousy inside Dylan. He managed to tamp it down, but only barely. His jaw ached from gritting his teeth.

Sawyer lowered Shelby back to the ground. "Hi, I'm Sawyer. Meg has told me so much about you. I'm glad you're okay."

Shelby was just looking at Sawyer with that stunned look women always got when looking at Sawyer. "Hi," she finally whispered.

Dylan rolled his eyes and crossed over to stand right next to Shelby, putting his arm around her shoulders. "Why don't you stop molesting your wife's friend and let her get dressed."

Sawyer put a hand up to his chest in mock woundedness. "Shelby is Megan's friend, which makes her like a sister to me." He winked down at Shelby. "A very hot sister."

"I am *so* telling Megan on you," Dylan said.

"Megan's used to my crazy antics." Sawyer shrugged. "Plus, she knows I am a one-woman man now."

"A tragedy," Shelby said, grinning.

Dylan had had enough. "You—" he pointed at

Shelby, spinning her around "—go get dressed. Call me if you need help."

"Or me." Sawyer raised his hand and wiggled his fingers in a flirty wave.

Shelby just smiled and went into the bathroom.

"You leave her alone," Dylan told Sawyer the moment the door was closed. The words poured out of his mouth almost of their own accord. "I'm not kidding about this, Sawyer. You stay away from Shelby."

Sawyer's face immediately changed from friendly to viciously serious. "You know what, Dyl? I'm going to let that slide because you've been through a lot in the past day and a half. And obviously you have some sort of head injury, because you just insinuated that I might be interested in cheating on my pregnant wife with one of her good friends."

Dylan rubbed his hand across his forehead. Sawyer was right. Dylan knew Sawyer loved Megan to distraction. He would never cheat on her or hurt her in any way.

"You're right. I'm sorry. It's been a long night and day and night again."

Sawyer was not one to hold a grudge. He slapped Dylan on the back. "No problem. So what the hell happened in here?"

Dylan told the whole story of Shelby's attack and the guy jumping out the window to kill himself.

"Do you think he traced our call?" Sawyer asked. "Is that why he was able to get here so quickly?"

"No. He was just following emergency services for this area. This is a small town and Shelby and I were a pretty big deal when we showed up alive."

"We're up against someone pretty serious if the guy was willing to off himself rather than be taken in," Sawyer murmured, looking around the room.

"My thoughts exactly. Definitely DS-13."

"I noticed our friend Shelby didn't seem to have any clothes on under that sheet. Please tell me the perp didn't rip them off her or something sick like that. Or worse."

Sawyer's voice was tight. Their family was intimately familiar with the trauma of aggravated assault and rape. Their sister, Juliet, had only just recently begun to fully recuperate from an attack while posing undercover a couple of years ago.

The Branson family took attacks on women very seriously.

Dylan cleared his throat. "No, um, Shelby's clothes were already off before he got in here."

Sawyer looked over at him, one eyebrow cocked. "I see. So your stupid comment before had nothing to do with protectiveness toward

Megan and everything to do with why Miss Keelan was naked."

"Shut up, Sawyer." Dylan loved his brother, but Sawyer knew how to push his buttons.

Shelby came out of the bathroom now dressed in Angi's pale blue sweater and jeans. She'd pulled her long red hair into a loose braid that fell down her back. And while Dylan appreciated that Angi's junior-size jeans were fascinatingly tight on Shelby's grown-woman-with-grown-curves body, he could tell right away that she was in pain from her leg. She tried to hide her limp, but Dylan noticed it immediately.

"I'm not sure these jeans are exactly legal on me." Shelby's laugh held an embarrassed tinge.

Dylan crossed to her and helped her sit down on the bed.

"Trust me, you look better in those jeans than any teenager ever could," Dylan said just loudly enough for Shelby to hear. She actually flushed.

Dylan shouldn't be surprised, given her skin coloring, that she was easily able to blush. But he was surprised at the crimson, given what had occurred between them this evening. Shelby wasn't used to compliments. Dylan might have to become better at giving them.

He bent down next to her to help her get her shoes and socks on so she wouldn't have to put undue weight on her leg. After he was finished, he gently touched the outside of her thigh where he knew it hurt the most.

"Are you sure you're okay?" Dylan asked, standing and helping her to stand. "We can still go to a doctor if you think we need to have it x-rayed."

"No, it'll be fine. Maybe just some aspirin or something once we get on the road."

"I'm going to go clear us out with the sheriff," Sawyer called from the door. He tossed a set of keys to Dylan. "I'll meet you guys in the car."

Sawyer and Shelby were both right. They needed to get going. DS-13 surely had more henchmen at their disposal to send once they figured out this one was dead. The next might already be on their way.

Dylan needed to get Shelby out of here.

They gathered the rest of their items, not that there was much. Just the contents of Dylan's backpack. Dylan helped Shelby down the outdoor stairs. He could tell she was in pain, although she didn't complain. He touched her bruised face gently once they reached the bottom, wincing.

"You have some bruises, too, you know, where that guy got in a few good punches," she told him.

Dylan could feel them. Between everything they'd been through over the past day and a half, Dylan's whole body felt bruised and sore. And he didn't even want to think about all the paperwork and mental energy he would have to spend dealing with the insurance issues surrounding his Cessna's crash. That would be dealt with later.

Right now he'd stay and make sure Shelby was safe. It wasn't as if he had any job to rush back to now anyway.

Dylan was helping Shelby into the car when Mrs. Morgan walked over to them. She had a bag in her hand.

"Here's Shelby's clothes, Dylan. I'm sorry you didn't get a chance to dry them."

"Thanks, Mrs. Morgan. Sorry our arrival has brought such chaos to your store. I'm sure Agent Branson will be giving Sheriff Fossen his card if you need anything further."

"Don't worry about that." Mrs. Morgan touched Dylan on his uninjured arm. "All this hoopla will bring in more people to the shop tomorrow than in decades. Angi is out taking pictures of the whole thing."

"You might want to consider getting her a real camera with her proclivity toward picture taking," Dylan said.

"I tried that. But part of the appeal for her is being able to put the pictures up on all her websites as quickly as possible." Mrs. Morgan shrugged then drew in a ragged breath. "I was so scared when that man put his gun to Angi's head." Mrs. Morgan leaned down so she could see Shelby more clearly in the car. "I'm sorry I told him where you were, honey. I just didn't know what to do."

Shelby reached out a comforting hand toward the older woman. "You did the right thing. A mother should always protect her child, no matter what."

"But those bruises on your face! I wish I had thought to tell him you were somewhere else."

"Mrs. Morgan, not to be gruesome, but that man was a trained killer. You're very lucky to be alive."

Mrs. Morgan's eyes got wider.

"He left you alive in that storage room for a reason—to check and see if you were telling the truth about where Shelby and I were," Dylan continued. "If you hadn't been, he probably would've come back and done a lot more damage."

Dylan decided it was probably best not to mention that the man would've almost definitely been coming back to finish off both Angi and Mrs. Morgan once he had taken care of business upstairs. One of DS-13's hired professionals would not have left loose ends.

"But thank you for coming up there with your shotgun, Mrs. Morgan," Shelby told her. "That was very brave."

Mrs. Morgan nodded. "You two be careful. Whatever's going on with you seems pretty dangerous."

"Yes, ma'am." Dylan nodded. "We'll be getting to a safer place soon."

"I better go make sure Angi is staying out of trouble."

They watched as the older woman walked back toward her shop, now surrounded by a number of flashing police cars and multiple bystanders, despite the late hour.

It wasn't long before Sawyer joined them back at the car. "Evidently this county doesn't have a lot of suicidal would-be killers. Go figure. Some of those deputies are just about giddy dealing with the crime scene."

"Do they need us?" Dylan really didn't want to stick around here to answer questions.

"No, since the guy jumped while being taken into custody and because the sheriff was right there to witness the whole thing, it's pretty straightforward. I told Sheriff Fossen I was taking you guys and how to get in touch."

"Were you able to get a good look at Shelby's attacker? He wasn't familiar to me at all."

Sawyer shook his head. "I saw him, but he wasn't familiar to me either. Didn't seem to have any identifying marks or tattoos on him. How long did you guys fight?"

"Over five minutes."

Sawyer's eyebrows shot up. "Any particular reason for that?"

"Well, I had been in a plane crash a few hours earlier. And I'm no longer active, Sawyer."

"So?"

Dylan knew what his brother meant. Dylan was particularly skilled at hand-to-hand combat. He'd been well known during his time at Omega for finishing skirmishes in under a minute.

"I was a little distracted by Shelby, but yeah, the guy was highly skilled. Definitely not a thug hired off the street."

Dylan and Sawyer both knew that was particularly bad news. Smart, skilled, hired muscle tended to speak of much smarter, more skilled people working behind them. In this case, someone very high up in DS-13, and perhaps even the mole in Omega.

They had no proof who was behind all this, they just knew it was someone connected and dangerous.

A lethal combination.

Chapter Seventeen

Shelby awoke in a bed, not sure exactly where she was. Definitely not at her own house. Light was coming through the window, so it was daytime, midmorning by the looks of it. Maybe she was in Sawyer and Megan's home. That would make sense. She moved quickly to get up, but a sharp pain in her outer thigh caused her to slow.

The last thing Shelby remembered was getting in the car with Dylan and Sawyer. They'd both sat in the front seat so Shelby could stretch out her hurt leg in the backseat. She'd been about to fall asleep when they had stopped at a drugstore for supplies for Dylan's wounded arm and painkillers for Shelby. And a couple of prepaid disposable cell phones to replace the ones they'd lost.

Evidently a respite from the pain had been all Shelby needed to fall asleep, because she didn't remember anything else about the drive into DC. She didn't remember the car stopping or getting into this bed or sleeping all night. But evidently all those things had taken place.

She was still dressed in Angi's jeans and sweater. She needed to go to the restroom and she was starving. Shelby took care of the first need then headed down the hallway to where she heard voices. Dylan and a woman. And the woman definitely wasn't Megan.

"Yeah, well, at least you don't look as bad as the time it was the two of us in the airplane hangar."

Dylan groaned and laughed at the same time. "Woman, that night just about killed me. Don't bring it up."

The woman chuckled in a knowing, intimate past-history way. Had Dylan brought Shelby to an ex-girlfriend's house?

Not a current girlfriend. Shelby didn't believe Dylan was the kind of man who would cheat on a lover. And especially wouldn't be stupid enough to bring the woman he was cheating with to his girlfriend's house.

But they were obviously close to each other. The familiarity between them was immediately apparent as Shelby entered the living room in which they sat.

Sat together, on a cozy love seat, in front of the fireplace.

It was the woman—a gorgeous brunette with

blond highlights—who saw Shelby first, to Shelby's continued chagrin.

"You're awake, good! Although I'm sure sleep was the best thing for your poor body." The woman stood and walked over to Shelby. She seemed unsure of whether to hug Shelby or offer her a hand to shake.

Evidently Shelby's facial expression wasn't real friendly-like because the woman ended up doing neither.

"Um, I'm Sophia Branson. This is my house. Well, mine and my husband's. I'm married to Dylan's brother Cameron."

This gorgeous woman was married to Dylan's brother. Thank goodness. But that didn't mean she and Dylan didn't have a history.

"Cameron? But you spent the night with Dylan in an airplane hangar?" Shelby could easily imagine just how well Dylan could get around in an airplane hangar with a woman. And he'd laughed and said it had almost killed him. The thought made Shelby a little sick. Dylan would know exactly what equipment could hold the weight of two peop—

The woman laughed, cutting off Shelby's thoughts of airplane-hangar antics. "Well, yeah. When a group of terrorists had me in their clutches. They used poor Dylan here as a human punching bag."

Both Dylan and Sophia winced.

Well, that wasn't what Shelby had thought at all. She shouldn't even have brought it up. Shelby stuck her hand out for Sophia to shake. "It's very nice to meet you. I'm Shelby Keelan. Thanks for letting us crash here."

Dylan came over to stand by his sister-in-law. "Sophia is the only member of our family who doesn't work at Omega. We thought it would be better for everyone else to go to work as usual. That will make it look like you and I aren't around this area at all, hopefully. After all, if we were here, we'd go straight to family, right?"

Shelby nodded. That definitely made sense.

"Plus, they're working on all the details for their grand plan to sneak you into Omega," Dylan continued.

"Do you really think the mole is someone inside Omega?" Sophia asked Dylan while she took Shelby's arm and began leading her into the kitchen.

"I don't know how it could be anyone else. It's either someone pretty high up inside Omega or someone with access to info he or she shouldn't have. That might be even worse."

Shelby agreed with Dylan's assessment, knowing how electronic leaks could be deadly to both companies and law enforcement. "Yeah, one mole would be better than having an unknown information leak. Something like that could be coming from hundreds of different electronic areas and would be nearly impossible to find."

"You have to be hungry," Sophia told Shelby as they entered the kitchen. "It's after eleven o'clock."

Shelby turned to Dylan. "How long have I been asleep?"

"Including your sleeping in the car? Almost fourteen hours."

No wonder she felt so groggy. And hungry. "Wow. Wait, what about the countdown I spotted in the coding?" Shelby instantly did the math in her head. "We have less than twenty hours left before whatever is counting down gets to zero."

Dylan slipped an arm around her shoulder. "I know. But you needed the time to rest. Plus, there wasn't anything you could do until we figured out how to get you into Omega."

Shelby was still feeling pretty anxious. As if there was something more she should be doing. But it didn't seem as though there was, so what could she do?

"Coffee?" Sophia walked over from the cabinet, carafe and mug in hand.

Shelby couldn't do anything else, but she could drink coffee. "Oh, please, yes. Thank you, please, yes."

Sophia laughed at Shelby's coffee enthusiasm.

"I'm the same way about coffee." She poured Shelby a cup, offered cream and sugar and went back to the kitchen counter and began making sandwiches.

"You should have seen the Branson siblings in here scheming away on the best plan to get you inside Omega with minimal detection. Megan and Evan were here, too."

"Evan is my sister Juliet's fiancé. They both are active agents like Cameron and Sawyer."

"You've got a pretty kick-ass family there, Branson," Shelby told Dylan after taking another blessed sip of her coffee.

"Well, the eldest sibling obviously got the biggest slice of the awesome, but the others do all right." Dylan winked at her.

Shelby completely ignored the little flip her heart did at Dylan's playful expression. Didn't pay it even one little iota of attention. Because that would be way too dangerous.

"I'm sorry I missed Megan." Shelby would have loved to see her friend right now.

Sophia turned from the sandwiches. "If I'm not mistaken, I think Megan is going to start having some 'pregnancy' issues and take a half day off work. She should be here not too long from now."

That sounded great. Because although Shelby liked Sophia, she needed a little time not around someone new. Not taking the mental energy to make sure she was being friendly and socially appropriate.

Megan didn't care at all if Shelby was socially appropriate. And actually, Dylan didn't seem to care too much about Shelby's quirky habits either. Neither of them were like her mother who seemed constantly flabbergasted by most of the words that came out of Shelby's mouth.

It wasn't as if she wandered around yelling profanity or racial slurs, Shelby just wasn't good at chitchatting and the social niceties that were so important to her mother and her mother's friends. Shelby just got straight to the point. And as far as Shelby could tell, her mother and friends never got to a point. Ever.

Sophia brought the sandwiches over and they all sat down at the kitchen table.

"So, did you all come up with a plan to get me in?" Shelby asked, then took a bite of her sandwich. Her eyes closed as she savored the bite. This had to be the best sandwich ever.

"Yeah, a good one." Dylan told her. "It's pretty complicated. They're building one ID for you to get you past front-desk security. Then a separate one to get you into the computer system. It won't fool the mole forever, but it should buy you and Megan a few hours to do whatever your wonder-twin powers can do."

Shelby stuffed another bite in her mouth. "Okay," she said, then cringed. *Never ever talk with your mouth full. Not even one small word.* Shelby had gotten plenty of smacks for that as a child.

But Dylan and Sophia didn't seem to notice. "We'll have to bring you in during the middle of the night when the least number of employees are around. Whoever the mole is knows we're alive, but doesn't know where we are," Dylan told her. "We'll use that to our advantage." He took a bite of his own sandwich.

"Do you really have all the numbers inside your head?" Sophia asked.

Shelby shrugged and nodded. She didn't like to make any sort of big deal about how she could remember numbers because it wasn't as if she did anything special. She just saw them and it was as though her brain took a picture. It didn't take any effort on Shelby's part, so she didn't like to take too much credit for it.

"Yes, she does have all those numbers inside her head. Plus every other number she's ever seen in her entire life." The words came from the hallway. Megan.

Shelby rushed over to embrace her quite pregnant friend. "Oh, my gosh, look at you, Megan. You're going to be a mom!"

"Yeah, tell me about it. I feel like a beached

whale. And I'm still mad at you for not coming to my wedding."

Megan turned her cheek up as Dylan came by, kissed it and helped her take off her coat. Then she hugged Sophia.

Shelby was glad to see her friend had found the big extended family she'd always said she wanted back at MIT. But Shelby did feel bad for missing her friend's wedding almost a year ago.

"I'm sorry, Megan. You know me and crowds of people. Plus, I was under a huge deadline then." The excuse sounded thin even to Shelby's own ears.

But Megan was not one to hold a grudge. "Well, you're here now and that's what matters."

Megan linked arms with Shelby and brought her back to the table. Sophia slid a sandwich in front of Megan, and Megan gave her a huge smile. "How'd you know?"

"Whether it's a boy or a girl, that kid already has the Branson appetite. You need all the food you can get."

Megan didn't disagree, just started eating. "Interesting little rule came into play at Omega today," Megan said in between bites.

"Oh, yeah, what's that?" Dylan asked.

"All persons entering the building must be checked for any electronic devices that could store significant data. No electronic drives of any kind are allowed through the front doors. Only items one hundred percent vetted and approved by a temporary cyberdivision task force will be allowed on the premises. Effective immediately."

"Have they ever done anything like that at Omega before?" Shelby asked.

"Nope." Megan wiped her mouth with a napkin. "And I don't know why they started today. It's pretty odd. Plus, I'm not on the cyberdivision task force, what's that all about?" Megan's irritation was plain.

"That is kind of weird. Do you think it has anything to do with us and the mole?" Dylan stood and walked his and Shelby's empty plates over to the sink.

Shelby jumped in while Megan was still chewing. "Did you tell anybody that I have the countdown codes in my head, Megan?"

"No, I don't think I explained your numeric photographic memory to anyone but Sawyer. It was just easier to tell the higher-ups that you had obtained the codes in a game. Why?"

"If I'm not mistaken, whoever is trying to kill me thinks the codes are on a drive. They have no idea they're in my head."

Dylan came back to stand beside Shelby. He put a hand on her shoulder. "That's right. When the guy attacked Shelby, he was asking her where the codes were. He thought they were on a drive, not inside Shelby's head."

Megan lowered her sandwich slowly back to her plate. "That explains so much. Whoever put out the directive for halting all hard drives and hardware from coming into the building is trying to keep us from bringing in the codes Shelby has."

"Do we know who sent out the directive, Megan?" Dylan asked.

"No, it was collaborative. Whoever the mole is did a good job convincing everyone at Dennis Burgamy's level and above that this was a necessary safety protocol, at least for the time being." Megan brought her sandwich halfway up to her mouth. "To be honest, as someone who works in tech, I can tell you it's not a terrible idea. We get all sorts of viruses and problems from corrupted drives and hardware that are brought in."

"But the timing is pretty suspicious," Dylan stated.

"Knowing that they think Shelby's data is on a drive, I would say the two can't be coincidences. There's just no way of knowing exactly where the directive came from without asking a lot of people a lot of questions."

Megan finished off her sandwich. "The good thing is, we don't have to get a drive inside the building. The mole is on high alert for technology. We've got something much better."

Megan reached across the table and grabbed Shelby's hand. "We've got Shelby."

Chapter Eighteen

What happened when you put five highly trained and industrious spies and a computer genius together and told them to figure out a way to sneak someone into the inner computer labs of a highly guarded top-secret facility?

This hugely complicated plan happened. That's what. Nothing with Omega was ever simple.

It was ten o'clock in the evening and they were sitting around Cameron and Sophia's living room after having had dinner together. The entire Branson clan—Dylan, Cameron, Juliet and Sawyer—were present, laughing, joking and figuring out a way to save the world.

Just like old times.

The plan was elaborate. Dylan's sister had created two separate false IDs and itineraries for Shelby. First, she would be Dr. Shelia Wonder, an American scientist who had been working in Australia, back to consult with Megan on some cyberterrorism research. Juliet knew the Omega computer and calendar system backward and forward from her time as an analyst. She'd already made it look as though Dr. Sheila Wonder had been scheduled to arrive tonight for months. Juliet's changes to the system wouldn't stand up to close scrutiny, but they would at least get Shelby through the door and past the guards.

"Seriously, Jules, Dr. Wonder from Australia? So that would be Dr. Wonder from Down Under?" Cameron teased his sister as his wife leaned up against him on the couch. He leaned over and kissed the top of Sophia's head.

"Hey, I wanted to make it something easy for Shelby to remember." Juliet winked at Shelby. "You've got enough to worry about. Plus, coming in from Australia gives Shelby a legitimate reason to be getting in and working in the middle of the night."

"Wonder from Down Under. I shouldn't have any problem remembering that," Shelby said.

"Dylan will be going in as your assistant. That might be a little more tricky since he used to work at Omega, but the guards on night shift shouldn't know him. You both just need to look exhausted and a little bit lost when you talk to the guards at the door. Megan will do most of the talking. Everybody loves her."

"That's true." Megan beamed.

Sawyer lifted his head from where it lay in her

lap near her belly so he could kiss her. "She's got that sexy-librarian thing going on."

"It's now just pregnant librarian." Megan rolled her eyes.

"You're damn sexy to me." Sawyer kissed her again.

Dylan saw Shelby smile. "Exhausted and lost won't be difficult for me."

"Once you're inside, you'll take on an entirely different ID. One that doesn't have anything to do with Megan. Whoever the mole is knows you're friends with Megan and might be looking for the two of you to go into the main lab together."

Dylan had to give it to his sister, she was a master planner. And she was just getting started.

"According to all electronic records, Dr. Wonder and Dr. Fuller—"

"Ahem, Dr. Fuller-Branson," Sawyer interjected.

"Pardon me," Juliet continued. "Dr. Wonder and Dr. *Fuller-Branson,* plus the assistant Dylan, will seem to be in the cybercrime unit, working on identity theft, a section completely removed from the main computer terminals."

"Your other ID will be a local police detective. No one of particular computer savvy or intelligence. You'll be going into the computer lab with Cameron. If anybody notices an electronic trace of that, it may seem a little odd, but won't draw attention like you and Megan coming into the lab together would."

"Megan will also be entering the room under a different ID, so you two can do whatever configurations you need to do," Juliet's fiancé, Evan, continued as Juliet linked her hand with his.

"It's all basically a bait and switch," Evan continued. "We're hoping the mole doesn't even know you're in the area and will focus his attention on trying to keep all electronic drives out of the building."

"But if the mole does think you're in the building, we're hoping they'll follow the Dr. Wonder path to cybercrimes. That will buy us more time," Juliet said.

Shelby looked over at Dylan, clutching at her arms, brows furrowed.

This was a lot for her, Dylan realized. Not just the plan—which, heaven knew, was complex enough to give anyone hives—but the being around all the people the way she had been all evening. Shelby didn't have any brothers and sisters, no real family except her mom. She wasn't used to the general craziness that came along with big families.

Dylan needed to get Shelby out of here. She needed protection right now just as much as she had against the attacker last night. His family was a different kind of threat. An unintentional and friendly one, but still a threat. At least to Shelby's mind right now.

Dylan moved closer to where Shelby sat propped against the couch. He didn't put his arm around her, but he did touch the back of her hand with his fingers. "Everyone else will be running interference as soon as Dennis Burgamy, their boss, arrives in the morning. If I had to guess, I'd finger him as the mole."

Dylan stood up and turned to his family. "All right, playtime's over." He reached down his hand and helped Shelby stand up. "Shelby needs some quiet away from you maniacs for a few hours. A chance to rest and focus on her role as Dr. Wonder from Down Under."

Dylan looked over at Shelby hoping she'd at least crack a smile at the corny joke, but if anything, her features were even tighter than before.

She'd stared down a poisonous copperhead snake yesterday and hadn't looked as frightened as she did now. He could tell his siblings and their significant others were all concerned for Shelby, but Dylan knew them voicing their concerns, or attempting to get Shelby to talk, would do more damage than good.

"We'll see you all at the scheduled rendezvous time in a few hours."

Dylan slipped an arm around Shelby's waist and led her all the way down the hall and into the bedroom where they'd slept last night. He deposited Shelby on the bed then turned to lock the door behind them.

Dylan sat down beside her on the bed, took her small hands that were closed into tight fists and rubbed them gently in his to get them to loosen.

"I don't think I can do this, Dylan." Her voice was barely a sound, even in the quiet room.

Dylan didn't know exactly what she meant by *this*. Pretend to be someone else? Break into a building? Figure out what the code was counting down to?

She turned away to look out the window. "I have an overstuffed chair in my condo, I've had it for years. It's old, and not very attractive, and my mother hates it with a passion. I jokingly call it my time-out chair. I go there whenever talking and people and life are too much for me. I just sit there and listen to the traffic outside, and that somehow reassures me that everything is going to be all right." Her voice got even softer. "I wish I had my chair here now."

Dylan wished she did, too. Anything that would help her feel less overwhelmed. He touched her hand again. "Let's try to break down what's making you feel uncomfortable, okay?"

Shelby nodded the tiniest bit.

"Anything with the codes and the computer

stuff?" Dylan didn't know exactly what she and Megan would be doing.

"No, that part I'm most secure about. I'm never wrong about numbers."

Dylan smiled slightly. He didn't doubt that.

"Is it pretending to be Dr. Wonder?"

Shelby shook her head. "No, I'm not going to win any awards for my acting, but I think I'll be okay."

"Then what?" he asked as gently as he could.

"I don't know if I can be around all the people, Dylan. Okay? It's been years since I've been in a building the size of Omega, full of people." Shelby's outburst took Dylan a little by surprise. And she wasn't finished. "I'm a very successful game developer, Dylan. I'm a millionaire because I'm good at what I do."

Dylan had figured out Shelby was a millionaire the first time she'd mentioned the game series she'd developed. "I know that, sweetheart."

"So I hire people, assistants, to do the stuff I don't like to do. That includes going anywhere there are a lot of people who would need to interact with me." She paused, then finally continued. "I can't hire anybody to do this for me."

"Shelby—"

"Dylan, I could barely be around your family, who are all very kind and nice and, holy cow, so darn in love with their respective others, for even a couple hours. How am I going to be able to be around an *entire building full of people*?"

She was shouting now, but Dylan didn't stop her. She stood up and turned to face him. Tears were streaming down her face.

"I can't do it." She brought her hands up to her face and began to cry in earnest. Dylan put both his hands on her hips from where he sat, but she took a step backward, shaking off his touch.

Dylan stood up and looked down at the tiny redhead so upset at the thought of having to *talk* to people. Dylan had to admit that he could not help smiling a tiny bit at the situation, but Shelby was obviously authentically upset and Dylan did not take her concerns lightly. He went and stood right in front of Shelby, gently running his hands up and down her arms.

"Shelby, you got run off the road, nearly run over by a car and were in a plane crash and you totally kept it together as if you'd done that every day of your life."

Shelby stopped crying a little, but didn't move her hands from her face. "But—"

"You got me out of a burning plane, saved us both from a poisonous snake, walked fifteen miles through the wilderness *in the rain* and then survived a pretty vicious attack. And kept focused and strong through all of it."

Shelby shrugged her shoulders, but at least

she took her hands down from her face. Dylan reached over to the bedside table and grabbed a box of tissues and barely restrained a chuckle when she gave the loudest, most unladylike blow he'd ever heard.

Dylan couldn't help it. He reached over and pulled Shelby up against his chest.

"I know you don't like people. It's okay not to like people." Dylan put his finger under Shelby's chin and tilted her head up to look at him. "And you know most of the people in the Omega building are not going to want to talk to you."

"I know." A flush crept across Shelby's cheeks with the adorable freckles. "I know my discomfort is stupid and ridiculous. But I can't help it."

"Hey, everybody's got their own demons. Yours aren't any less real than mine just because I don't fight the same ones." Dylan couldn't help himself, he dipped his lips down and kissed her. "We've come this far. Don't give up now."

A tiny little sigh escaped Shelby. "I won't give up. I'll do it. I know how important this is."

"*You* are what's important," Dylan murmured against her lips. "And I will be with you the entire time. We'll all be there to help you and run interference where needed. Especially in the chitchat department. That's dangerous stuff."

"I'm sorry I threw a fit." Shelby's crooked smile was perhaps the most adorable thing Dylan had ever seen. "My mom never knew what to do with me growing up when I would get so hysterical about being around new groups of people. She was a social butterfly and loved interacting with everyone and trying to show me, and my ability to remember numbers, off."

"I can't imagine that went over well."

"Yeah, I could never be the socially adept daughter she wanted. Our relationship is pretty strained even to this day, although she doesn't like to admit that."

Her mother's pressure that Shelby be gregarious around crowds probably had only complicated and multiplied the discomfort she had about being around people. Dylan had such a loving, supportive relationship with his family, it hurt him to think of Shelby never having something like that.

"I know you haven't had a great experience with family, but you can trust, unequivocally, that my family has your back. Okay? If you get into a situation at Omega and you're panicking, you let one of us know and we'll help you get through it."

Shelby reached her arms up around his neck and pulled his lips down to hers. "Thank you," she murmured.

"For what?"

"For not calling me crazy. For not writing me off. For having faith in me."

There were things Dylan wanted to tell her, but

they got lost as Shelby walked forward, forcing Dylan to step back until his legs were against the edge of the bed.

Dylan wrapped his arms around her hips and brought them both down to the bed. Their hands became more frantic, removing clothes as quickly as possible. Their lips only separated from each other when they had to in order to remove clothes. Dylan peeled Shelby's jeans down her legs, careful of the one that was still tender.

Oh, holy hell, she was wearing that black-and-red thong. And a very wicked grin.

All thoughts of the dangers and risks they would take later that night disappeared. All Dylan could think about was Shelby and this moment.

And that thong.

Chapter Nineteen

Dylan walked into Cameron and Sophia's kitchen to make a pot of coffee. It was just two o'clock in the morning, but they were all going to need the caffeine to get through the next few hours. Evidently most of his family had headed back to their own homes for a few hours of rest, since the living room was empty.

But his sister was sitting at the kitchen table.

"Got any more of that?" Dylan asked Juliet, pointing to the mug of coffee in her hands.

"I think the pot is just about empty."

Dylan nodded and began to make more. "Everybody head out?"

"Yeah. Megan needs as much rest as she can get, so Sawyer took her home. Evan wanted to be at Omega already, to make sure everything looked clear."

Evan and Juliet had both been known for keeping highly irregular office hours at Omega, even before they'd become a couple. Security wouldn't bat an eye at seeing either of them there in the middle of the night. After all, bad guys didn't work just nine to five, so good guys couldn't either.

"This is a pretty good plan you've come up with, sis."

Juliet handed Dylan two cell phones. "Here's a couple of phones for you and Shelby in case you need them." She took another sip of coffee. "Let's hope my plan is enough. It's hard to hide when you don't know exactly who you're hiding from."

"My money is on Dennis Burgamy as the mole."

Juliet shrugged. "Burgamy is a general pain in the ass and perhaps the greatest kiss up who's ever been involved in law enforcement. But a traitor? I just don't know, Dylan."

Dylan shrugged. "Well, whoever it is, we're going to need to be ready. Once they figure out we've got Shelby and her numbers into the system, it's going to cause them to move into action quickly."

"Where is Shelby, by the way?" Juliet asked.

Dylan didn't quite meet his sister's eyes. "She's in the shower. She'll be out in a minute."

"She seemed a little overwhelmed earlier. She going to be okay?"

"Shelby doesn't do well around a lot of people. Tries to avoid it as much as possible. So the thought of going into an entire office building full of people is a little traumatic for her."

"Because she's afraid they'll attack her or arrest her or something?"

"Um, no. Actually, I think her greatest fear is that they'll all want to talk to her."

"Talk?"

"Yeah, like chitchat." Dylan smiled and poured himself a cup of coffee. "Honestly, I think she'd prefer it if they were chasing her or shooting at her."

"Okay, then, we'll be sure to protect her from all the dangerous talking."

"She's not crazy, Jules."

"I'm not mocking, I promise. You're talking to the woman who slept on a closet floor for a year and a half because of the terrors I had built up in my mind. Fears are fears whether they seem legitimate to other people or not."

Dylan knew Juliet understood fears all too well.

"Shelby will be all right. Once we get her in with the computer system, it'll be like a playdate for her and Megan."

Dylan smiled just thinking about Shelby with access to the technology Megan had created at Omega. Dylan hoped he was around to see the pure geek joy. He smiled into his coffee.

Dylan looked up to find his sister staring at him. "Oh, my gosh, Dylan, you're falling for her."

The statement totally caught Dylan off guard.

"No." Dylan used his best this-discussion-is-over tone, but Juliet just ignored it the way she always had.

"I would warn you off, but the way she was looking at you this evening—like you were her lifeboat and she had no idea how she would survive without you—I think she's falling for you, too."

Had Shelby really been looking at him like that? No. Juliet had to be mistaking Shelby's panic for something more romantic. "Look, Shelby and I have had a traumatic couple of days. Yeah, it's led to a little sex, but that doesn't make it something serious." And if it did, Dylan definitely did not want to talk about it with his little sister.

Juliet laughed, obviously enjoying Dylan's discomfort. "Are you kidding? You guys were all over each other with the little touches here and there all evening long. You even carried her dishes over to the sink for her."

"She has a hurt leg, Juliet. I was trying to be a gentleman like Mom raised me to be. Besides, you guys were touching each other all night, too. You're like the poster children of PDA."

Dylan saw the trap he'd set for himself as soon as the words were out of his mouth.

"Because we're all *in love*, Dylan. It's just natural. And notice how you and Shelby just fit right in with the rest of us."

Dylan shook his head. Hoping his silence would clue his sister in. It didn't.

"Is this about Fiona and the baby?" she asked.

Dylan groaned. "No. It has nothing to do with her."

"Dylan, I'm going to say this because it's time. I know Fiona was your wife and I know what happened to her was a tragedy and that we're not supposed to speak ill of the dead…"

Dylan raised his eyebrow when Juliet hesitated. He couldn't remember Juliet ever talking about Fiona before. "Yes?"

"Well, Fiona was kind of a shrew."

Dylan barely avoided spewing the sip of coffee he'd just taken.

"I know what happened was sad, especially because of the baby, but you can't stay frozen in that place any longer, Dylan. You don't want to do law enforcement anymore because of what happened, that's fine. We all support you and none of us blame you. But you've got to stop closing yourself off from the rest of the world."

"You're one to talk, Jules."

"Look, don't throw how I handled the rape back in my face. Yeah, it took some time, but I had to come to the same place you're going to eventually have to come to—I could choose to let one moment control the rest of my life, or I could decide my own destiny. I chose Evan. I chose love."

Dylan was so proud of the corner Juliet had turned lately in her personal life. She'd struggled for so long and Dylan was glad she'd found happiness. But… "It's not the same, Juliet. This is just a casual thing between Shelby and me. We'll both be going our separate ways in a couple of days when this is all over."

"You keep telling yourself it's a fling, big brother. And when you wake up a few months or a year or whenever from now and you realize you let the perfect woman slip through your fingers because you were too blind to do anything about it, well, then you remember this little cup of coffee we had tonight."

Something in Dylan's heart clenched at Juliet's words. Because yes, Dylan could very clearly picture himself waking up in the middle of the night and reaching for Shelby and her not being around. And that frightened him more than anything else had for a long time.

But Dylan didn't have time to think about this right now. There were other much more important things that needed to be done tonight. Sorting out his feelings for one tiny, gorgeous, quirky, freckled female was not one of them.

So Dylan didn't care if both his tone and his words were a little harsh. He just needed to shut his sister up—damn her for always being able to see too much anyway—so he could focus on the mission at hand. Dylan set his coffee cup down with a resounding thump on the table and told his sister the exact opposite of what he was feeling.

"Whatever, Jules. I have no plans to ever see Shelby Keelan again when this is over. There's nothing real between us. Nothing special. She's just another woman." There, that should shut Juliet up for a while.

He'd expected an angry or annoyed look from her, but when Dylan glanced up he saw his sister look over his shoulder into the doorway of the kitchen and cringe. Dylan didn't have to turn around to know.

Shelby was there and had just heard his statement.

IT WAS ALWAYS good to have things spelled out for you with utter clarity just to make sure you didn't have any delusions of romantic grandeur for the man you'd just had sex with. Shelby would've said *made love*, but that evidently was too strong a phrase for what she and Dylan had shared.

And whatever real connection she'd felt with Dylan, whatever passion and tenderness she thought she had seen in his eyes earlier? Those were evidently figments of Shelby's overactive imagination.

Shelby would've eased back out of the kitchen, but Juliet had already seen her. Had already given her that oh-I-am-so-sorry-men-are-such-jerks look. Which Shelby would've appreciated more if said jerk wasn't two feet away from her.

"Shelby—" Dylan turned toward Shelby with an arm outstretched.

Shelby left a large distance between his hand and her body. If he touched her now—if anybody touched her now—she would shatter into a million pieces.

"Is that coffee? Thank goodness. There was no way I was going to make it through this night without coffee." Her voice sounded tight even to her own ears.

But she wasn't sobbing on the floor as she really wanted to do, so she'd just call that a win.

Not that she had any reason to be sobbing. Dylan hadn't promised her anything. The opposite, in fact. He had told her that he didn't do serious relationships. Had basically announced he was still in love with his dead wife.

Everything that had happened between them had been based on adrenaline and their hazardous circumstances. Fate had thrown them together, they'd been attracted and they'd acted on that attraction.

No harm, no foul.

It wasn't until Shelby actually heard Dylan say

that what they had was nothing real or special that she realized she'd been hoping for something different when this crisis was all over. Maybe not a ring and promises of forever, but definitely not "no plans to ever see each other again."

Ouch. But it was better to know, right? To know that Dylan thought so little of her, of what was between them?

Shelby realized she'd been staring at the coffee-pot without moving for an unreasonable amount of time. The silence at the table behind her was deafening. She picked up the pot and poured some into her mug. Damn it, now she was going to have to turn around.

And look at Dylan. And not cry.

Shelby would give ten years off her life for some sort of witty, socially acceptable thing to say right now. Why hadn't she listened and learned from her mother?

"Good, everybody's up. I'm leaving to go to Omega in a minute. Everybody good?"

Shelby closed her eyes briefly in relief and turned around. It was Cameron, with no knowledge of the awkward situation floating around the kitchen. He came over to get a cup of coffee, giving her shoulder a friendly squeeze.

"You ready for this, Shelby?"

"More ready than I was five minutes ago, that's for sure. Time to get this done so you all can stop some bad guys and we can all move on with our lives."

"Shelby—" Dylan stood and began walking toward her.

"I've got to get my Dr. Wonder outfit on that Juliet provided for me. It won't take long." Shelby grabbed her coffee mug and began to leave, giving Dylan a wide berth.

"I'll come with you," Juliet said.

"No, that's not necessary." Shelby did not want to talk about what Dylan had just said.

"Just in case you have any questions about tonight, Dr. Wonder, that's all." Juliet linked her arm with Shelby's, brooking no refusal.

In the bedroom, Shelby turned and locked the door. She didn't think Dylan would come in, but wanted to make sure.

"I mean this strictly professionally, although in undercover work personal matters definitely come into play. Are you okay?"

Shelby looked over at the bed where she and Dylan had just been an hour before. No, she wasn't really okay. She deliberately turned her back to the bed.

"I'm going to get the job done. That's what really matters, right?" Shelby got the trousers and blouse out of the closet.

"It does matter. But it's not the only thing that matters, Shelby."

"Look, your brother never promised me anything, Juliet. We've only known each other for forty-eight hours, for goodness' sake, so what he said in there—"

"He didn't mean." Juliet was quick to cut Shelby off. "He was irritated with me and was trying to shut me up, so he said something obnoxious."

Shelby snuffed out the tiny piece of her heart that wanted to grab hold of Juliet's words. It didn't matter *why* Dylan had said the words, he'd still said them.

"You don't have to defend him, Juliet. Like I said, how involved can two people be after just two days?"

It sure felt a lot longer than that to Shelby, but she wouldn't mention that.

"Getting these numbers in my head into Megan's computer, figuring out what the countdown is leading to and where it will happen, that's the most important thing now. Hurt feelings between Dylan and I are pretty insignificant in comparison."

Juliet grinned at her. "Are you sure you've never worked undercover before? You sound like a seasoned pro."

Shelby slipped on the outfit to make her into Dr. Wonder. The blouse was a pale tan and the pants were a darker tan. They were as nondescript as you could get. "You probably won't still think that the first time I actually have to talk to people."

"You're going to do fine. Just let Megan or whoever you're with do most of the talking whenever possible," Juliet told her.

Shelby ran an exhausted hand through her hair before pinning it up in a bun to look like the professional PhD she was supposed to be.

Somehow she was afraid saving the world from a terrorist attack was going to be the easy part of the next few hours.

Chapter Twenty

"I see it's on the schedule, but I don't know why you're working this late at night, Dr. Fuller-Branson. You should be home getting your rest."

Shelby had been both completely ignoring Dylan and watching sweet, pregnant Megan charm the four guards at the front entrance of the Omega building for the past five minutes. Except she wasn't really charming them, she was just being herself. She knew each guard by name, asked each about their families and any ailments they may have ever mentioned.

Shelby was in awe of her friend. Having gone to MIT with Megan, she knew the woman was a genius, but Megan was able to interact and talk with people—put them at ease and make them feel important—in a way that was totally foreign to Shelby.

And it wasn't an act. Megan genuinely cared about others. Shelby cared about others, too, but was always so awkward and stiff that interchanges rarely went the way she intended.

"Michael, I went home and rested all afternoon," Megan assured the guard. "You know there's no way Sawyer would stand for it otherwise. I wouldn't be surprised if he showed up in a little while anyway."

All the guards nodded, smiling, in approval of Sawyer's good husbanding. Shelby barely refrained from rolling her eyes. It was a good thing Megan wasn't one of the bad guys, because she probably could've gotten away with just about anything without ever even raising a weapon.

"Besides, Dr. Wonder and her assistant have flown all the way from Australia to work in the cybercrimes lab. It's the middle of the afternoon for them."

If Shelby didn't know it was Dylan standing next to her—sexy, virile Dylan—she might never have given him a second look. He had somehow contorted his posture until he looked unassuming and nonthreatening in any way. He definitely didn't look like the confident, strong man Shelby had seen wrestle an unwieldy plane safely to the ground or defeat her attacker. The ill-fitting suit, glasses and horrible slicked-back hair helped the ruse, but it was Dylan's demeanor that sold it.

For the first time, Shelby could understand just how good Dylan had been at undercover work.

The guards glanced at Shelby and Dylan and nodded politely; one of them handed her a visitor's badge with her name and info on it, but their concern was for Megan. Shelby was a little disappointed that not a single one of them made the Wonder from Down Under joke.

"I know you guys have extra security we need to go through. No drives, right?" Megan asked them, handing them her purse to go through the X-ray machine. Shelby and Dylan in turn handed over their purse and briefcase as well.

"Yes, ma'am." The guards all looked a bit sheepish. "Plus, we now have this new body scanner everyone has to walk through. They brought it in yesterday afternoon."

Whoever was trying to keep out a drive with all the numbers on it was doing a pretty thorough job. No one would be able to get any computer equipment or drives past that scanner.

"Um," the first guard spoke up again. "We already asked to make sure it was safe for a pregnant woman."

Megan's smile was obviously sincere. "Thank you, guys. I really appreciate it."

They walked through the scanner, one similar to the new fancy security scanners at large airports, individually. Everyone was deemed clear to pass.

"See you later, guys. Have a good night," Megan said.

Shelby and Megan moved quickly toward the elevators, Dylan one step behind.

"That's quite a fan club you have there," Shelby told Megan while they waited for the elevator doors to open.

"Elevators have cameras," Megan whispered as the door opened. "But yeah, they're all wonderful guys. Most hoping to be full agents one day."

They rode up in silence. Dylan kept his head down and pretended to be shuffling through some files he held in his hands.

"There are cameras in the elevators, but not the offices or hallways," Megan told her once they got out. "Sorry, should've mentioned that before." Megan shot a worried look at Dylan.

He nodded. "Yeah, we just have to be as alert as we can. We couldn't prepare her for everything."

Something as simple as making a joke in the elevator could bring down this entire operation. Shelby suddenly became very aware of how precarious everything really was.

"My plan is just not to talk to someone I don't know unless I need to."

Megan wrapped her arm around Shelby as they walked down the hall. "Aw, honey, that's always your plan." She kissed Shelby on the cheek. "And I love you for it."

Megan knew what it felt like not to fit in. That's why Shelby had bonded with her so completely.

Shelby was very aware of Dylan on the other side of her and the huge distance between them. She hadn't talked to him directly since what she heard from him in the kitchen. As far as Shelby was concerned, there really wasn't anything left to be said.

Dylan had said it all.

They made it to the cybercrimes office, which was empty at this early hour.

"Okay, as soon as we scan our IDs into this door, the clock is on. The Omega system will think we are all in there. That will only fool the mole for as long as there are no human eyes checking on us. If the mole is as high up as we're afraid he is, that will only take a phone call once people start reporting in."

Shelby nodded. That gave them a few hours, hopefully.

"I know I'm being monitored because you're my friend and I'm the computer guru. What helps us is the mole probably thinks we're spending all our effort trying to get you into the building with some sort of hard drive."

The elevator pinged down the hallway and Shelby startled in the quiet. Dylan slipped his arm around her to offer support, but Shelby shrugged it off.

It was Juliet's fiancé. That's right, Evan was providing them the second set of IDs.

This cloak-and-dagger stuff was already wearing on Shelby and she'd only been doing it for five minutes. She had no idea how people worked undercover for weeks at a time.

"Here's your local police IDs." Evan handed another set of scanner cards to Shelby, Dylan and Megan.

"Won't they realize these IDs didn't come through the front door?" Shelby asked.

Megan nodded. "Yes, that's possible, but it's two different systems. Someone would have to cross-reference the two."

They all looked at each other. That was a danger and they all knew it.

"Juliet's plan is good, but the best it does is open us pockets of time. You and I are going to have to work fast, Shelby," Megan said. It was three o'clock in the morning. At best they only had three or four hours. It wasn't going to be easy.

Shelby nodded. She was ready. Especially if it meant she didn't have to talk to Dylan.

Megan scanned the IDs for Dr. Wonder, Dylan and herself into the cybercrimes lab door. "Okay, that's it. We're officially on the clock. The mole is most definitely going to be watching for me. Hopefully he'll think I'm here in the cybercrimes office as long as possible, since my ID won't check in anywhere else."

"Let's get you two to the real computer lab," Evan said. "Cameron should be waiting for us there."

They walked through a series of hallways and used the back stairs instead of the elevators to avoid cameras. The whole building seemed dangerous in its partial darkness. To Shelby, it felt as if eyes followed them everywhere, that at any time someone would jump out. She didn't want to be attacked out of the blue the way she had been while lying unawares at Mrs. Morgan's house. She shuddered at the thought, the pain in her leg becoming more pronounced.

"You okay?" Dylan asked.

Shelby desperately wished she could lean into his strength. To just take a second and breathe in Dylan's calm and feel his arms fold around her.

But that had also been stolen from her while she was lying unawares. Shelby just didn't want to be attacked anymore.

"I'm fine," she told him.

But Dylan wasn't willing to let it go. He grabbed her arm as they walked. "Shelby, what you heard—"

"I don't want to talk about it, Dylan." She tried to snatch her arm away, but that was laughable when Dylan didn't want to let her go. Although she noticed nothing about his grip hurt.

Evan and Megan glanced back at them from their place in front, then sped up to offer Shelby and Dylan a bit of privacy. Privacy Shelby didn't want.

Dylan slowed them down so Evan and Megan pulled away even farther.

"What I said to Juliet in the kitchen was just to get her to shut up, Shelby. She was pushing my buttons and I said the most obnoxious things I could think of."

"We don't have any promises between us, Dylan. I know that. We're just a fling, noth—"

Shelby didn't even get the words out before Dylan stopped them both and backed her up against the wall. Hard.

And kissed her until she was breathless and clinging to Dylan.

He pulled back from her and cupped her face in his hands. "Damn it, Shelby, I know this isn't the time. I know there are bigger things at stake here than you and me. But I couldn't let you go one more second without you knowing how sorry I am for what I said. None of those words were true."

Dylan grabbed her arm and they began walking again at a quicker pace to catch up with Megan and Evan. Shelby now had no idea what to think.

She wasn't sure if she should still be mad at Dylan or if what he said was the truth.

She wasn't even going to think about it right now. She didn't know if she would ever think about it again. And then it didn't even matter because they were at the door of the main computer lab. Cameron was waiting for them.

"Should both Cameron and Evan be here? Will that be suspicious?" Shelby asked.

"No, there would always be at least two Omega employees here with anyone from the outside. The only thing that is really suspicious is that it's three o'clock in the morning. But we didn't have much choice about that," Cameron explained.

"You ready?" Megan asked her. "Everything okay?" She looked pointedly between Shelby and Dylan.

"Yes." Shelby nodded. "It'll take me a little while to enter the numbers in, Megan."

"That's fine. The system will begin analyzing them as soon as you're done." Megan collected the second set of IDs from Shelby and Dylan to scan them at the door. "Let's hope this works."

"Many Bothans died to bring us this information." The words were out of Shelby's mouth before she even realized it. Megan gave her an odd look, but Shelby didn't take offense. Megan didn't get most pop culture references.

"It's go time," Cameron said to Evan. They actually bumped fists.

Megan and Shelby both rolled their eyes. "*It's go time?* Seriously?"

"Hey, you just quoted *Jedi*. Don't give us a hard time," Evan said, laughing. He scanned his ID at the door.

"All right, here we go. We're on clock number two now," Megan said, scanning the other IDs. Cameron followed up with his.

All joking stopped. If Shelby didn't get these codes out of her head and into Megan's system before the mole figured out they were here, then everything would be for naught.

Shelby turned to Megan. "You know what it will be like for me while I'm entering in the data. Don't stop me, even when it's ugly. If I don't get it all the first time, I won't have the time to recoup and do it again."

Megan nodded and squeezed Shelby's hand.

Shelby was glad Megan understood. Shelby had to do this no matter what personal price she paid. Because if she didn't, they'd be too late to stop whatever the DS-13 countdown was for.

Chapter Twenty-One

Shelby, behind a keyboard, was amazing.

Dylan had never seen anything like it. Her fingers flew on the numeric keypad as she stared blankly ahead typing numbers from inside her mind that only she could see. She'd been doing that for over an hour.

"That's pretty freaky, man," Evan said from where they both stood at the back of the room. They spoke in hushed voices, but Dylan didn't think Shelby would notice them even if they were yelling.

Dylan had known Shelby was good with a keyboard because of her success as a video game coder, but this was almost like a superpower. She never stopped, never made a mistake, just typed in numbers at the fastest pace any of them had ever seen.

"I don't think I could type numbers that fast even if I was randomly pressing buttons," Dylan said.

And that she was remembering all of these in her head? That was beyond amazing.

Megan came over and sat down in one of the conference chairs near where they were standing. "She's pretty amazing, isn't she?"

Dylan nodded. Yes, she was amazing, but he'd known that before she started typing. He just hoped he hadn't screwed up any chance with her whatsoever.

What a stupid mess he had made in the kitchen. The look on Shelby's face. Dylan hoped to go the rest of his life without ever seeing that look on her face again.

Because what they had was special and she definitely wasn't just another woman. Dylan looked at Shelby now, and the things he felt were both terrifying and thrilling.

And even though he had no idea what to do or what sort of future they might have, he hoped to God he hadn't ended the entire thing by something said so carelessly.

"You know, DS-13 embedding their information in a children's internet game is pretty impressive. Brilliant, actually," Megan said.

"With an organization as widespread as theirs, it's a pretty effective way to communicate. They can get different levels of information to different people. No phone calls to be recorded or emails that can be traced," Evan continued.

This game was popular amongst grade-school children. A help-the-detective-type mystery. The game was unique in that it was only available once a week on Saturdays for only one hour.

Now that they knew what DS-13 was hiding in the coding of the game, they understood why it wasn't constantly available.

It was much more possible that someone would've found the pattern if the game had been continuously available. Not likely, but possible. So they'd only made the game—and thus its coding—available one hour per week.

"Shelby started following the game to get ideas for her own games. She likes to watch games in their code form because coding is in numbers and that's how her mind works." They all watched Shelby while Megan talked. Yeah, it was obvious her mind worked differently—more brilliantly— than theirs when it came to numbers.

"The game can't be recorded or played back, the coding deletes itself after just a moment, so I'm sure they were feeling secure in what messages they were sending out in the games," Megan continued. "Because who would've ever believed that there was someone who could not only recognize that there was some sort of message going on inside the game, but also someone able to memorize the entire sequence after only seeing it once."

"The good guys caught quite a big break with Shelby," Cameron muttered.

"And we better use that to our fullest advantage. This could really be what we need to begin to bring DS-13 down completely," Evan agreed.

Dylan left them to talk and walked closer to Shelby. What she was doing was obviously taking a toll on her. She continued her constant data entry, but her lips were now tightly pursed and her face was paler than before.

"Shelby needs a break," he said to Megan as she came to stand beside him. "It's hurting her to do this. Why?"

"Have you ever given one hundred percent of your focus to one thing for an extended period of time? It's like using the same muscle over and over. At first it's fine, then it's tiring, then it's agonizing. That's probably the point she's getting to."

"Then she needs to stop. Stop her, Megan."

Megan laid a hand gently on his arm. "She wants to finish, Dylan. She knows we have a limited amount of time."

But in just the couple of minutes that they'd been talking, Dylan could tell Shelby was feeling worse. Her breathing was becoming labored. Dylan was horrified to see her nose begin to bleed on one side.

"We have to stop this," Dylan said.

"Give her a few more minutes. She's got to be

close to finished. If we stop her now, she may not be able to get herself functional enough to restart and finish in time."

Evan and Cameron joined them. "Is it just me or is Shelby not looking so good? Is that blood?"

Evan's words were enough. Dylan was putting an end to this. He began walking toward Shelby, determined to stop her.

Megan—moving pretty darn fast for a little pregnant lady—got in front of Dylan before he could reach Shelby.

"Megan, look at her." Shelby was now trembling. Color had washed out of her face. But her fingers kept moving.

Megan put a hand on his chest. "It hurts me, too, Dylan. She's my friend. But she asked me to make sure she was allowed to finish."

"Have you ever seen her like this? At school?"

"Not this bad, no," Megan admitted.

Dylan looked at Shelby again where she sat at the computer terminal. He closed his eyes. "I have to stop her."

"Her body will stop her if it gets too bad— she'll pass out. It's the mind's way of protecting itself from unmanageable pain."

She shouldn't have to go that far. Dylan had no idea it would be this way. "Did Shelby know this would happen?"

"She knew it wouldn't be comfortable."

Wouldn't be *comfortable*? This was so far past that.

"She knows what's at stake, Dylan. It's DS-13. They're known for incurring as many casualties as possible in their attacks. It's a countdown and information that went out to every DS-13 operative. Whatever that countdown is to, it's *big*."

"I know that, Megan, but look at her!" Both nostrils were bleeding now and her shoulders were stooping. Dylan gently, but firmly, moved Megan out of his way. He couldn't watch this anymore.

But Megan grabbed his arm. "If the roles were reversed and you had the chance to stop DS-13 even though it meant pain to yourself, wouldn't you want the chance to do it? Don't let her suffering be in vain. Respect her enough for that."

Dylan stopped. Megan was right.

And he did respect Shelby's strength.

Though she be but little, she is fierce.

But Dylan would give anything if he could take some of the pain racking her small body into his own right now.

Shelby began to slump forward, tears rolling down her cheeks from eyes that were still closed. Dylan rushed over to her to hold her up, to lend his strength in any way possible. Her fingers kept plucking away at the numeric keypad.

"You can do it, sweetheart. Hang on." Dylan whispered the words in her ear. He felt her lean against him, so he wrapped both arms around her. He could feel her weakening.

Her fingers abruptly stopped their movement. Shelby's eyes opened. Her breathing was labored as she looked over at Megan, then Dylan.

"Done." Her voice was nothing more than the hoarsest whisper.

Dylan caught her as she fell to the side, completely unconscious. As gently as he could, he swung her up in his arms. Megan quickly sat down in the seat Shelby had vacated at the main computer terminal.

"She got it all in. Amazing." The wonder was clear in Megan's voice. "Is she okay, Dylan?"

Dylan sat in one of the other chairs, keeping Shelby clutched against his chest. There was no way in hell he was letting her go. "Her breathing is less labored, a little bit of color coming back into her cheeks." Evan handed Dylan a tissue and he used it to wipe the blood from Shelby's nose.

"Now I just need to allow the software to run the configurations of the data Shelby entered. It won't take long and we'll know what the countdown was leading to and where."

Shelby's eyes began to blink and then opened. "Did I finish?" Her voice was still a whisper.

"Yes. You were amazing." Dylan kissed her

forehead, thankful that she wasn't trying to get out of his arms. Because he didn't think he could let her go. "Megan is running the configurations now."

Shelby nodded wearily. "Good, because there's more."

"More what?"

"It doesn't matter, they're later. We've got to worry about the imminent countdown right now."

Dylan wasn't sure what Shelby was talking about. He wasn't sure she knew what she was talking about. So he didn't push it, just held her.

Shelby brought the hand she'd used on the number pad up and cradled it to her chest. Her fingers were extended at odd angles.

"My fingers are cramping."

Dylan took her fingers between both of his and began rubbing gently. He wasn't surprised they were cramping at the rate she had been using them. She whimpered a tiny bit at his ministrations, but didn't pull away.

Megan was busy at the keyboard providing further instruction to the software she had created, feeding info back in when it was needed. Dylan just held Shelby while all this went on and watched as strength began to creep slowly back to her body.

Dylan could feel the exact moment when that strength tipped the scales and caused Shelby to remember that she shouldn't be sitting in his lap. He watched as her green eyes went from soft to shuttered right in front of him.

For the first time in a very long time, Dylan remembered what it was like to feel his heart crack. He hadn't let anyone close enough to do that sort of damage in years.

Shelby stiffened and began to sit up and move away. Dylan let go of the fingers he was rubbing and didn't try to stop her, although he stayed close by in case her sudden strength deserted her.

Shelby walked over to the terminal where Megan sat. Numbers were scrolling across the screen like something out of *The Matrix*. Dylan had no idea what any of it meant. He could tell Evan and Cameron didn't either.

Shelby put her hand on Megan's shoulder and Megan touched her hand gently in acknowledgment, but neither woman took their eyes from the screen.

"There."

Both women said it in unison. Shelby pointed to a group of numbers on the screen and Megan nodded. Megan began typing something else.

Across the room a phone rang. Cameron went to answer it, but Dylan knew it was bad news. Nobody would be calling this room at this hour except a member of his family with information they didn't want to hear.

"We're running out of time, ladies," Dylan told them.

"We're almost there." Megan kept typing as she spoke.

And then, as suddenly as Shelby's had, Megan's fingers stopped moving. Both stared at the screen, then looked at each other, horror clear on their faces.

"What?" Evan barked. "What is it?"

"The countdown is for a bombing here in Washington, DC." Shelby's voice was once again hoarse as she turned to look at Dylan. "Set to go off at eight thirty this morning."

That was a little less than two and a half hours from now.

"Where in DC? Do you know?" Dylan crossed to Shelby and put his hands on her upper arms. She looked as if she might collapse again.

"On the Mall, right in front of the Lincoln Memorial, in a maintenance tunnel."

A monument, even the Lincoln Memorial monument, wasn't too bad. An artifact, even one as important as this, could be rebuilt. Lives couldn't.

"Okay," Evan said. "That's not as bad as it could be."

Now Megan spoke up. "No, it's much worse.

There are children's groups, elementary schools from all over the country performing at the Mall this morning. It's been all over the news. It's called Celebrating America's Future."

Dylan's jaw clenched. It was the most perverse and perfect target a group like DS-13 could think of. Attacking a celebration of *America's future*. DS-13 had probably been waiting a long time for something with such a degree of poetic justice.

"We'll stop the kids from coming in, keep them all out of the Mall area," Evan said.

Shelby shook her head, looking at Dylan. "The kids are already there, most of them have been there since three or four o'clock this morning. Part of the program begins at sunrise." Shelby grasped onto Dylan's arms. "They're planning to attack our children."

Chapter Twenty-Two

"Okay, things just got more complicated." Cameron hung up the phone he was on and ran over. "Burgamy just arrived at Omega. Juliet's calling in the bomb squad and FBI. We'll meet them at the site."

"What the hell is Burgamy doing here so early?" Dylan asked. It was highly suspicious. Especially when taking into consideration the DS-13 plans they'd just discovered. Did he want to be here so he could have a front-row seat to the destruction and death his organization was attempting to cause?

"There's more, in the codes, more information," Shelby said. "Did you see it?" she asked Megan.

"No, it was going by too fast."

"Was it stuff about today, Shelby?" Cameron asked. "We can't waste any more time. Unless there is more information about today, we've got to get to that bomb."

"Yes, I think. Maybe a way to disarm the bomb. I'll keep checking." Shelby's face was pinched.

Dylan walked to Evan and Cameron by the door. Evan was already back on the phone with Juliet providing her with all the info Shelby and Megan had given them.

"You guys need to be careful about any mass evacuation of those kids," Dylan told Cameron. "DS-13 could be watching and might trigger the bomb early if you try something like that."

Cameron nodded. "You need to stay here with Shelby and Megan, Dylan. Buy them the time they need to access whatever they can from those codes. Them finding a disarm code may be our only chance."

Dylan nodded. He knew he could do more good here than at the bomb site. There would be other people, much more qualified people, who would take care of that situation. And if the mole knew Megan and Shelby were pulling info about DS-13 from this computer location, he would be coming to eliminate them.

Dylan had no intention of letting that happen.

But Dylan also knew he was sending all his siblings, and one of his best friends, Evan, into potentially the deadliest situation they'd ever faced.

Dylan hugged Cameron. "You be careful and get everyone out of there alive."

"You do the same, big brother."

Evan slapped Dylan on the shoulder and followed Cameron out of the room.

Dylan turned back to the women. It was just a matter of time before they were found in this room. Who they were found by would determine the next course of action.

Megan was staring at the door Cameron and Evan had just run out of. Her face was ashen. "They're all going, aren't they? To the bomb site."

Megan meant Sawyer. She didn't say his name, but Dylan knew who she meant.

"I didn't even get to say good-morning to him," Megan said softly. "We always find each other whenever the later one gets to the building. To say good-morning. Always. We've never missed even once."

Dylan met Shelby's eyes just for a moment. Shelby was concerned about her friend's distress. Dylan was, too. Since Megan had a genius IQ, Dylan would try to appeal to her reason.

"Megan, it's an emergency. I'm sure if Sawyer could've—"

Dylan's words were cut off by the door flying open. It was Sawyer. He rushed over to his wife and put his hands on both her cheeks.

"Good morning." He kissed her tenderly, briefly, then put his hands on her pregnant belly for just a moment. "I'll see you later tonight at home. I promise."

Sawyer said nothing else, just turned and ran out of the room, slapping Dylan's back on the way out.

Dylan saw Shelby wipe away tears at the tender scene between his brother and Megan. Megan, who a moment ago seemed distraught, now was focused and secure.

"Let's get back to work," she told Shelby, pulling up another chair at the terminal. They immediately began sorting through numbers and information on the screen. Dylan didn't even pretend to understand what they were doing, just let them work.

Dylan knew what his job was. Protecting them from whoever walked through that door next, although he wasn't sure how he would do that with no weapon, no credentials and no authority. But the person who came through the door a few minutes later was not who Dylan was expecting.

Chantelle DiMuzio, Dennis Burgamy's personal assistant, walked in. Her head, as it almost always tended to be, was stuck in her electronic organizer.

"Oh, sorry, am I in the right room?"

Chantelle had started working at Omega after Dylan had left, so he didn't know her well. But he had met her a couple of times, most recently last year when helping out on a mission involving Juliet and Evan.

"Hi, Chantelle, I'm in here." Megan threw up her arm and waved, but didn't get up from her seat at the computer terminal.

"I'm Dylan Branson, we've met before," Dylan said to the woman.

She seemed a little harried. Although she worked day in and day out with Dennis Burgamy, Dylan was a little surprised she wasn't constantly pulling all her hair out. Not only did Dylan think the man was the mole, Burgamy was also just a jerk in general. Nobody got along with him.

"Yes, I remember," Chantelle told him. "And you look just like your brothers."

She flushed a little at that. Evidently Burgamy's secretary had a little crush on one or both of Dylan's brothers. She wasn't the first, Dylan was sure. He decided to up the flirt factor, keep Chantelle talking about nothing for as long as possible.

"You're here early. I hope they pay you overtime for hours like this."

Chantelle rolled her eyes. "I wish. I'm salary, so no overtime no matter what."

"And you have to work with Burgamy all the time? That's a little cruel and unusual."

Chantelle looked down again. "I thought you had been in a plane crash."

Damn. "Yes, I was, but fortunately made it out alive."

"Oh, well, that's good. I didn't know that, but

here you are." She gave him a smile, but didn't look him all the way in the eyes. "Mr. Burgamy said you had a woman with you, too, that she was bringing in some sort of numbers on a hard drive or something. Is she okay?"

"She was fine, too. Unfortunately, the hard drive was destroyed." Dylan hoped that information would be passed along to Burgamy. Give him a false sense of security about Dylan's being here.

"It was destroyed? I don't think that was reported to Mr. Burgamy's office yet."

"Sorry. One of my siblings was supposed to have done it yesterday, I think. They're such slackers." Dylan gave her his most engaging smile.

Poor Chantelle didn't seem to know what to do with Dylan's charm. She looked back down at her computer tablet. "Um, the computer log showed this room as being used by Cameron and Evan with guests. But then the front-door log showed that they just left the building. So I was just trying to figure out what was going on."

Now Megan stood up and walked over. Dylan didn't know how they would explain any of this. They didn't want to tell Chantelle anything about the bomb because that information would go straight to Burgamy.

"Evan and Cameron were here, but they had to leave. So I came in here," Megan told the other woman.

Chantelle really looked confused now. "Oh. Because the system says you're logged in to the cybercrimes offices with a Dr. Wonder. It doesn't have any record of you in here."

Megan caught Dylan's eye. Neither of them were sure what to say. "Yeah, the system must be glitching or something. I can look into that. I'm multitasking right now. Back and forth everywhere."

Something beeped on Chantelle's computer. "Okay, that's Mr. Burgamy. He's already here and on a rampage about something." She typed furiously. Then looked over at Shelby at the computer. "You guys didn't bring any hard drives in here, right?"

For just a second, Chantelle wasn't a frazzled, worn-down employee. She was taking in and weighing everything in this room.

"Are you kidding, Chantelle?" Megan laughed and linked arms with the other woman. "Nobody can get in here with any drive of any sort. Have you seen the new crazy security machine they have at the front doors? I felt violated just walking through it."

At Megan's words, whatever Dylan had thought he saw in Chantelle was gone. She was back to frazzled, overworked employee with a terrible boss, barely able to take her eyes off her computer tablet.

"All right, if you guys are okay in here I'll just leave you to it. But I'll have to call a couple more agents to come in, Megan, because of the rules about visitors."

"No problem, Chantelle. Thanks. Sorry for your early morning."

Chantelle nodded and was already walking out the door, answering her phone and typing at the same time.

"Well?" Dylan asked.

"I think it's only a matter of time before Burgamy knows we're here. I didn't want to ask Chantelle to lie to him. It didn't seem right and would look suspicious since we don't have solid proof about Burgamy."

"I agree." Dylan looked over at Shelby, who was still frantically working on the computer. She was slowed down by having to use her left hand to type and enter data. Her right hand was still clutched against her chest.

"There's a lot more information in there than we thought," Megan said. "Shelby's looking for stuff concerning the bombing specifically right now, but there's other info, too. Important intel on DS-13. It's a huge breakthrough, Dylan."

Dylan nodded. "But right now, we've got to focus on the bomb. Anything that you can find to help them."

"Believe me, I know." Megan nodded and made her way back to where Shelby worked.

A few minutes later, four Omega employees entered the room. All size large. None of them looking personable.

The muscle had arrived. If Burgamy decided to put an end to the work Shelby and Megan were doing, Dylan wouldn't be able to stop all four men before they stopped the women.

Dylan gave a half grin at no one in particular. He may not be able to stop them, but he'd damn well try. Dylan slipped off his suit jacket so it wouldn't hinder his movements if quick action became necessary.

"I'm sorry, but I need to ask all of you to allow us to do a scan of your clothing and possessions," Big Guy Number One said.

Shelby looked over at Dylan for the first time. He nodded. She stood up so the man could use the scanner to eliminate any doubt that she had any electronics on her person. The same was done to Megan and Dylan.

One of the other guys reported in the finds— that all of them were clean—but Dylan didn't know to whom. Burgamy? Chantelle? Did it mean anything? The men then scattered around the room, casually but strategically.

Dylan doubted he'd be allowed to leave the room now even if he wanted to.

A few minutes later, a smaller man, obviously not muscle, entered the room. Where Megan had pretty much ignored the big guys except to submit to their scans, this person she paid attention to.

"Hello, Dr. Fuller-Branson. You're working early this morning," the man said in a singsongy voice, ignoring Dylan and the other men and crossing directly to the computer terminal. Everything about him screamed computer geek. Dylan was surprised he didn't have a pocket protector.

"You, too, Dr. Miller. I'm surprised to see you here." Megan's response was clipped. It was the first time Dylan had ever heard Megan be less than overtly friendly with someone.

There was no lost love here.

"I've been asked to come in and check that there are no contraband hard drives being used in the system."

"Asked by whom?" Megan demanded.

"Burgamy's office. If you must know." Miller's voice was just as rigid as Megan's.

Megan glanced over at Dylan, one eyebrow raised. Dylan gave her a small nod. He was becoming more and more convinced that Burgamy was the mole. They just needed to figure out a way to prove it.

"Fine, Dr. Miller. Check away. We have no external drives."

Miller thoroughly vetted the computer. Looked

in places Dylan had no idea you could even attach an external drive. The man seemed genuinely shocked not to find one.

"You really don't have one?"

"No." Megan shrugged. "I told you that."

"Megan, where is this data from if not a drive?" The man's curiosity had obviously outweighed any ill feelings he had toward Megan.

"Jim, I know you and I have had our differences, but this is important. We're the good guys here. But—" Megan looked around casually at the men sitting in the room and lowered her volume "—perhaps not everyone in this building is."

Miller looked at Dylan, then back at Megan and Shelby. He nodded. "I'll let them know that there's no hard drive. But I'm supposed to stay here and report on what you're doing."

Shelby and Megan were already back at work, both of them frantically scanning data. They were running out of time with the bomb.

And with Dr. Jim Miller here to report on every move they made, things had gotten just about as bad as they could get.

Or so Dylan thought.

Because then Dennis Burgamy walked through the door.

Chapter Twenty-Three

Shelby heard somebody else enter the room behind her and cringed, gritting her teeth. It was getting really crowded in here.

She knew things were falling apart around them. That the mole—Burgamy or whatever his name was—was closing in. Maybe the computer would be taken away at any moment. Heck, for all Shelby knew, maybe they were all about to be thrown into some dark cell or killed.

She could hear talking going on all around her, could feel all the people, but tried to stay focused. She had finally found the thread she was looking for, the one that would lead to the code needed to disarm the bomb.

What time was it? How much time did they have left before the bomb went off?

All the voices in the room were driving Shelby crazy. She wished she could poke her fingers in her ears. But her right hand wasn't working anyway, still cramping every time she tried to move it, so that couldn't happen. She was already feeling sick from the effort to get the data in earlier. She needed quiet. She needed to be alone.

Damn it, she needed to know what time it was.

"Dylan." Shelby knew he was talking to someone, could hear their voices louder than the rest. But Megan was too busy talking to the other computer guy who came in to ask her.

Dylan was by her side in just a moment. "Hey." He brushed a strand of her hair out of her eyes. "You okay?"

She was so tired.

"I've almost got what I'm looking for—the code to shut off the..." Shelby trailed off. She wasn't sure if she was supposed to say anything in front of these people. She had no idea who was good and who was bad anymore. "What time is it?"

"Almost eight o'clock. Keep working, okay?" He kissed the top of her head and Shelby almost believed that he cared. "Everyone is waiting for our call."

"I've found the right string. I just need a few more minutes to follow it."

"Okay."

"It's getting crowded in here, Dylan. That's hard for me." Shelby desperately wanted Dylan to understand. She wouldn't be able to function for much longer.

Somebody said something from across the room, but Dylan held out an arm to silence the person. He crouched down next to Shelby, giving her all his attention. "Shelby, I know how hard this is for you." His words were whispered so no one else could hear. "You've already been so strong, baby. Keep it up just a little bit longer, okay? Get that code for my family to dismantle the bomb and I promise I will get you away from people for as long as you want."

Dylan did understand. He didn't think she was making stuff up just to get attention, as Shelby's mom had always felt.

Shelby nodded and turned back to the monitor. Using the last of her strength and focus, she pushed all the voices and presence of others to the background.

She saw the trail she was looking for in the massive amount of code. She began to follow it, reading the numbers the way most people read books.

She only needed one small group of numbers. She knew they were there. But it was like finding one particular sentence in the middle of a large legal document. Even though you knew what to look for, it was hard to find.

But people, *children*, were going to die if Shelby didn't find that code.

So she shut everything out and focused.

There. There it was.

"I've got it," Shelby announced.

"She's got what? What has she got?" Shelby heard the angry words from behind her, but didn't know who said them.

"Go, Shelby, I'm ready," Dylan said, also ignoring the man who was yelling.

Shelby read off the eight-digit code. She looked over to find Megan with her cell phone also. Both she and Dylan were sending the code to the bomb site.

"Anything else they need to know?" Megan asked.

"No, that's it, according to this data."

Shelby sat back and spun the chair away from the computer terminal for the first time since she'd sat down in it. There really were a lot of people in here. No wonder she had been going a little crazy.

One guy in particular, Shelby had to guess he was Burgamy, based on what she had heard, was pretty livid.

"Why the hell didn't you notify me that you were here, Branson?" Burgamy asked Dylan. "And are you okay from your crash?"

"My plane did go down, but we somehow managed to survive. We somehow managed to survive a lot of things over the past few days."

Burgamy's eyes narrowed at that. "I'm not sure

what's going on here, Branson, but we have pro-tocols and rules that have to be followed. Perhaps you've forgotten that in the years since you've last worked here."

Burgamy didn't show any signs of stopping his tirade anytime soon. Shelby wasn't sure how long she could listen to him before she did or said something really inappropriate.

She just needed to get out of here for a while. As far as Shelby could tell, neither Megan nor Dylan had heard anything back from the bomb site. That was a good thing, right? Shelby hoped so, because she didn't think she could get back on that computer with all this human nonsense going on around her.

Chantelle DiMuzio, the lady who had been here earlier, came back in the room.

"Chantelle, why wasn't I notified that Dylan Branson was in the building? I thought he and Ms. Keelan had critical information that we needed."

"I did update the status report when I found them here earlier, sir. But Mr. Branson informed me that the hard drive with the data they were meant to deliver had been destroyed in transit, so I lowered their rank of importance in the sys-tem." Chantelle's voice was tight but level. Ob-viously she was used to this sort of conversation with her boss.

"At least you sent in some other Omega employees, as per protocol." Dennis Burgamy straightened his tie. Obviously protocol was the most important thing to him.

Shelby *really* didn't like that man.

She could feel something inappropriate building inside her. If she punched Burgamy, would she be arrested for attacking an officer of the law? Did that law still apply if the guy was obviously a total jerk? Shelby actually took a step toward the man.

It was Chantelle who stepped in and saved the day. She set her tablet down on the table and turned to Burgamy. "Sir, these ladies have been in here all morning working. It looks like they need a break. If it's okay, I will escort them to get some coffee and will stay with them the entire time."

Burgamy hesitated and then nodded. "Fine. I want to talk to Branson anyway. About, for example, why none of his siblings seem to be here today."

Shelby looked over at Dylan and he nodded. Shelby sure hoped Burgamy was the mole and that Dylan would find a way to prove it or else it looked as if all the Branson siblings were going to be looking for new jobs.

Megan and Shelby followed Chantelle out the door.

"Thanks for getting us out of there, Chantelle," Megan said as they walked down the hall. "I think

Shelby had had all she could stand and might have been about to do your boss bodily harm."

"Dennis can be a little much sometimes," Chantelle said.

"A little much?" A gross understatement, if Shelby had ever heard one.

"Okay, a complete pain in the ass most of the time," Chantelle snickered.

All three women laughed.

"How well do you know Burgamy, Chantelle?" Megan asked.

"We've worked with each other every day for four years and I constantly ask myself why I don't quit." Chantelle laughed again, shaking her head. "Hey, do you gals want to get coffee at the place next door instead of the break room? I could use a little fresh air."

Shelby could, too, and they readily agreed. It didn't take them long to work their way out of the building.

Shelby barely refrained from throwing her arms out and spinning around once they made it outside. She finally felt as if she could breathe. There was nobody around her and all she could hear was the sound of traffic and construction.

It was like music to her ears.

Shelby knew she had done a good job. She had gotten all the data in the system and she and Megan had found what they needed to stop the bombing.

She'd been an important part of saving a lot of lives today.

She and Megan would figure out what the other parts of the code meant and hopefully put a stop to even more of DS-13's plans.

But Shelby also knew this meant that she and Dylan would be going their separate ways soon.

She'd accepted that he hadn't really meant what he said in the kitchen. Dylan wasn't cruel; he wouldn't say something unkind to hurt her purposefully, even if he didn't want to continue whatever was between them. But the fact was, they hadn't made any promises to each other, and it didn't seem likely that Dylan was going to be ready to make any promises anytime soon.

If there was one thing Shelby knew from programming, it was this: timing was everything. She and Dylan had the chemistry for sure, and cared about each other. But the timing wasn't right.

Shelby was brought back into the present by Megan linking arms with her. "Did you hear Chantelle's suggestion?"

"No, I'm so sorry, I was in a different world."

"There's a new coffee place that opened the next block over that has fabulous chai tea. Chantelle thought we could try it out."

"Sounds great to me."

Actually, nothing sounded great to Shelby, but she knew she was just going to have to move on. The wind picked up. She wished she had a jacket.

"Let's cut through this alley," Chantelle said. "It'll get us out of the cold quicker."

"Good. I'm freezing," Megan said, grabbing Shelby's arm more securely.

"So what were you guys working on so hard in there? Shelby looks like she's been through ten rounds," Chantelle asked. "It's such a shame that hard drive was destroyed. There weren't any other copies?"

"Not to speak of," Shelby said.

"So I came to realize when I checked you out a little further, Shelby…" Chantelle said.

Megan and Shelby both stopped walking. Shelby realized the wind wasn't whipping around them any longer.

Because Chantelle had led them down an alley that had no opening on the other side. It was a dead end. And there wasn't another soul around.

Chantelle didn't even look like the same woman who had been up with them in the computer lab. This woman wasn't browbeaten by an overbearing boss. She was someone very much in control.

And she was someone pulling out a gun and putting a silencer on the end of it.

"You're the mole, not Burgamy," Megan said.

Chantelle rolled her eyes. "Burgamy is a sycophant and a moron. He doesn't have enough intelligence to play both sides. Especially not to work for DS-13."

Chantelle pointed her gun at Shelby. "You. I can't believe someone like you, who can hardly have a coherent conversation with more than one other person, is the one causing DS-13 so many problems."

She twisted the silencer the rest of the way onto the muzzle of the gun. "I spent too much time trying to keep any sort of hard drive out of the building. I thought that would be enough. Shame on me for assuming. But honestly, who even knew that someone like you existed? Someone with all the codes *in her head*. Freak."

Shelby and Megan looked at each other, but said nothing.

"I want you to take out your phone and call Dylan," Chantelle continued. "Tell him you made a mistake with the bomb-disarming code and that you just figured out it was wrong. Give him a new number to relay to his siblings."

"No," Shelby told her. "I don't care if you shoot me. I won't do it."

"Oh, but, Shelby," Chantelle said with a half smile that almost looked friendly. "I won't shoot you. I'll shoot Megan here. Right in the belly."

Chapter Twenty-Four

Dylan watched Burgamy dismiss three of the four guards that had been posted in the room. Dr. Miller had ducked out as soon as possible after the women left. That left one other Omega employee, Burgamy and Dylan.

Dylan had no plan to leave Burgamy alone in this lab with the computer if he had any other option.

"What's going on, Dylan?" Burgamy asked. "Where are your siblings?"

Dylan knew he couldn't tell Burgamy anything. Hopefully, Burgamy had no idea that they knew about the scheduled bombing. Dylan didn't want to give him the opportunity to tip off DS-13 before the bomb unit and his family had a chance to disarm the bomb.

"I don't know where they are." Dylan shrugged. "I don't work in law enforcement, so they're not at liberty to tell me all of their whereabouts."

Burgamy rolled his eyes. "Fine. I'll deal with

them later. Tell me what was going on in here. Why would you sneak in here? You've walked through the doors like you own the place enough times."

Maybe it was time to start putting a little pressure on Burgamy. "I just thought it was pretty interesting that the first time I pick someone up for Omega, *both* engines on my plane suddenly fail."

"It was sabotage?"

Dylan nodded. "Somebody trying to kill Shelby Keelan and make it look like an accident. But you know what's even more interesting? There were only a few people who knew *I* would be the one flying her in."

"What are you trying to say, Branson?"

"I'm not trying to say anything. I'm just pointing out some facts the way they happened."

"What? Are you kidding? When Chantelle and I heard that you had made it out of the crash alive, I was thrilled. You can ask her. I wasn't sure why you hadn't reported in."

Something wasn't right, Dylan realized. When he first talked to Chantelle this morning, she had said she thought he had crashed. Then asked about the hard drive. Why would she do that, unless…

Dylan's phone began to vibrate. He took it out of his pocket.

Shelby. Calling him. On the burner phone they had bought. He distinctly remembered her aversion to talking on the phone. She'd even let him listen to her voice-mail message while they had joked at Sally's that first night: *Sorry, I can't take your call. Please hang up and text me.*

Shelby Keelan did not talk on the phone if she had any other option.

"Hey, Shelby. Everything okay?"

"Hi, Dylan."

Dylan could tell immediately that Shelby was on speaker and outside. "Are you outside? Where are you?"

"Um, yeah, Dylan. We're just going to get coffee at that new place around the corner. Look, this is important. Do you mind reading back to me that number I gave you earlier to pass along to your brothers and sister and the bomb squad."

Puzzled, Dylan grabbed the notepad and read them back to Shelby.

"Yeah, that second-to-last number isn't right. I'm so sorry, Dylan. I just made a mistake. It should be a three not an eight. I feel so terrible making a mistake on something so critical. It's really important that you call them and let them know I made a mistake."

"I will, Shelby. You don't worry about it, okay. Just go enjoy your coffee. I'll see you soon."

The phone instantly cut off.

"Will you please tell me what the hell is going on?" Burgamy roared.

Dylan had been wrong about Burgamy. He wasn't the one who worked for DS-13.

Chantelle DiMuzio was. And she had Shelby and Megan.

"Your assistant is a double agent for DS-13. And there's a bomb in DC about to kill a bunch of people if Omega doesn't stop it."

Burgamy's curse was vile. "I knew we had a leak, but I didn't know who." Burgamy cursed again. He walked over to the other Omega employee still in the room. "I assume you're carrying?"

"Yes, sir."

"I need your weapon right now."

The man handed it to Burgamy. Burgamy turned and handed it to Dylan.

"Let's go get Shelby and Megan. And take that bitch Chantelle down," Burgamy told him.

Dylan was already running out the door. He went straight past the elevators to the stairs and began taking them two at a time.

"I assume your siblings are already at the bomb site? Don't you need to call them?" Burgamy asked between breaths. The older man hadn't seen active duty in a lot of years, but he was managing to keep up.

That was good, because Dylan wasn't going to wait for him.

"No."

"I thought Shelby told you to call them. What were those numbers you were writing down?"

"They were nothing. Shelby was buying time and Chantelle was trying to make sure the bomb goes off."

"Are you sure?" Burgamy questioned.

"Absolutely." Dylan had no doubt, especially after what he'd seen her do today. "Shelby never makes mistakes with numbers."

Dylan made it out of the staircase and sprinted through the main lobby. He could tell the guards were going to stop him. He slowed, not wanting them to shoot him by mistake.

"I am Director Dennis Burgamy. Clear the path for this man!" Burgamy yelled it while swiping his badge for Dylan to get out the front door of Omega.

Dylan took back every bad thing he had ever said about Burgamy.

Outside, Dylan was unsure which way to go and stopped. Burgamy came up behind him.

"She said they were going to the new coffee-house. But Chantelle wouldn't take them to a pop-ulated place."

"The new coffee place is around the block, ac-tually behind the building. If you could get there from the alley next door, it would be great. But I don't think that leads anywhere."

Which would make the alley a perfect place

to take two people if you were trying not to be seen or heard. Dylan took off running toward the alley, praying he wasn't too late. Burgamy was right behind him.

"We need to take her alive if we can, Branson."

Dylan nodded, but he wasn't willing to make any promises. He forced himself to slow down and be more calculating with his movements. Rushing up on Chantelle guns blazing would do nothing but get Shelby and Megan killed.

Dylan turned back to Burgamy. "Let's split up. I'll go down this side of the alley, you work your way down the other side. Stay a few paces behind me."

Burgamy nodded. "Alive, Dylan."

"If she's hurt Shelby or Megan then I promise nothing."

"Fair enough," Burgamy muttered then crossed to the other side of the wide alley.

Dylan dashed from blockade to blockade, trying to move as quickly as possible, but not do anything to tip off Chantelle that he was there. He was thankful for the Glock Burgamy had provided for him.

Although he couldn't see them from this angle, Dylan finally got close enough to hear someone speaking. Chantelle. Still talking with Shelby and Megan.

For the first time since Dylan realized a murderous operative who had fooled trained agents for years had Shelby in her clutches, he felt as if he could breathe. Shelby was still alive. Dylan would make sure she stayed that way.

"I see that it's after the scheduled time for the bombing and it still hasn't detonated. You may have stopped this attack, but I'm going to make sure you don't stop any more," Chantelle was telling them.

"There's going to be a lot of suspicious people when we were last seen with you and our bodies are found in an alley." Shelby didn't sound scared. She sounded mad.

"That's so naive of you. But you don't have to worry about anybody finding your bodies here. Someone from DS-13 will be along to clean that up five minutes after I let them know you're dead."

"It won't work, Chantelle." Megan sounded decidedly more frightened.

"Of course it will work. I've been working undercover for DS-13 for years with Omega. You know what the key to my success was? Not trying to do too much. I wasn't trying to bring down Omega. This wasn't personal. I didn't help every bad guy and criminal organization that came along. I just did a little slip of information here and a tiny drop of false information there. I've gone undetected for years, and I'll continue to do so."

Dylan peeked for a brief second around the corner of the garage container that hid him. He instantly broke out in a cold sweat. It was like something out of the nightmares of his past. An assassin, a gun and a silencer.

Pointed straight at the woman he loved.

No. Dylan could not lose Shelby this way. Dylan knew he'd promised Burgamy he'd try to take Chantelle alive, but that just wasn't going to happen.

"So I'll just finish you two off and go in and wipe all the data Shelby entered. You may have stopped today's attack—and after all the planning that went into that, I'll be a hero with DS-13 for killing you—but you won't be around to stop anything else."

Dylan steadied the Glock in his hand and got ready to jump out. He didn't have a great shot at Chantelle from this angle, but he wasn't going to sit here and do nothing. Not again.

One, tw—

"Drop it, Chantelle!"

Dylan heard Burgamy's words and dived out, firing as soon as he could see Chantelle. She was startled and fired her weapon right at the women, while turning to fire at Burgamy. Shelby screamed and leaped at Megan, trying to pull her out of harm's way.

Dylan's first bullet hit Chantelle in the shoulder. He squeezed off two more rounds that hit her in the heart. Chantelle fell dead to the ground. Both Shelby and Megan were crying, which reassured Dylan.

"Burgamy, are you hit?"

"Yes." The older man bit out the word from where he lay on the ground. "But I'll live. I'm calling it in. Check on the women."

Dylan ran over to Shelby, who was crying hysterically now, sitting on the ground near Megan. Blood was all over their clothes.

"The baby, Dylan. Megan's been shot. The baby. Just like your baby. Oh, no!" Shelby was inconsolable.

Dylan's heart stopped. He looked over at Megan, who was obviously still alive, but covered in blood. Megan couldn't lose the baby. Please God, no.

"Megan." Dylan rushed to her side where she sat on the ground. Her face was as ashen as Shelby's. "Where are you hit?"

"Dylan, nothing hurts except my butt where I hit the ground when Shelby grabbed me." Megan's voice was shaky. She took a couple of deep breaths as Dylan started pressing along Megan's body to try to figure out where she was hurt.

"Dylan!" Megan said loudly. "I just felt the baby kick. The baby's fine."

Then where was all this blood coming from? Dylan and Megan both looked over at Shelby, who had her hands over her head and was rocking back and forth.

Dylan put his arms around Shelby. "Shelby, listen to me. Megan is fine. The baby is fine."

Shelby refused to be consoled. "No. I saw the blood."

Dylan looked down at Shelby's beige blouse. The blood was definitely coming from Shelby. "You got shot, Shelby. Not Megan. You did."

"What?" Shelby finally stopped sobbing.

Dylan put his forehead directly against hers and began trying to find her wound. "Megan is fine. *You* are hurt."

"The baby's okay?"

Dylan nodded.

"Megan's okay?"

Dylan nodded again.

"You're okay?"

Dylan rolled his eyes. "Yes, we're all okay. You're the one who's hurt." And at the rate blood was beginning to drip from her blouse, Dylan was seriously becoming concerned. He laid Shelby down against the pavement. Her face was waxen, her skin was clammy. Her breathing more and more labored.

Dylan ripped open her blouse to see the wound. It had gone in the fleshy part of her side, but might have nicked her kidney at the rate blood was rushing. Dylan tore off his shirt and began pressing it against the wound.

"Burgamy, we need a medic back here, stat. I mean, like five minutes ago," Dylan yelled out. He heard the man relay the info.

"Dylan, I don't feel so good," Shelby muttered.

"Hang in there, baby. If you don't, I'm going to call you and make you talk on the telephone every day for the rest of your life."

Now Megan was crying. "She pushed me out of the way, Dylan. If she hadn't…"

Dylan didn't say anything. He didn't have to. Both he and Megan knew if that bullet had hit Megan in the same area it had hit Shelby, the baby would be dead. Megan probably, too.

Dylan could hear reinforcements running down the alley. He kept his hand firmly pressed on Shelby's wound. "Help is almost here. You stay with me, okay?" Dylan put his head right next to Shelby's.

Shelby's green eyes looked up at Dylan, but he didn't think she really saw him.

"Dylan?" Shelby whispered.

"Yes, Freckles?"

"I promise I won't die."

Dylan leaned down and kissed her tenderly. "I'm going to hold you to that promise."

Chapter Twenty-Five

Shelby kept her word and didn't die, but it was touch-and-go for a couple of days. Days of agony and soul-searching for Dylan. He refused to be moved from the waiting room while the doctors operated on Shelby to repair the damage the bullet had done to her kidney, stop the bleeding and save her life.

His family joined him one by one in the waiting room as they came back from the scene of the would-be bombing at the Lincoln Memorial. The bomb had been shut down, dismantled and removed from the location without any fanfare. Omega Sector didn't need glory or accolades from the press. They just did their job and got out. The public didn't need to know how close they had flirted with disaster.

Dylan's family sat with him in the waiting room, as the one small woman who had done the biggest part to save thousands of lives, fought for her own.

When the doctors came out to give a report and asked if they were family, everyone gave a resounding *yes*. Shelby was theirs now, regardless of whether Dylan decided to pursue her or not.

The doctors weren't hesitant to let the Bransons know how close a call it had been. Just an inch farther... Just a minute or two more... The picture that *could have been* was bleak. And they all were thankful it wasn't what it could have been.

Burgamy was also in the hospital, a bullet to the shoulder. Nothing life threatening. The man had already sent down his regards and well wishes for Shelby. Dylan was glad he had been wrong about Burgamy. The man may have been a pain in the ass, but at least he was one of the good guys.

Once Shelby stabilized and began waking up, Dylan's family left. It had been a long, exhausting couple of days for everyone. Juliet was the last one to leave.

"Do you want to come home and get a little rest? Take a shower?" she asked Dylan.

"I will. After I've talked with her. Made sure she's okay."

"You sure you don't want to tell me she's not important again? Just another woman?" Juliet's eyebrow was raised.

Dylan couldn't even joke about it. "I will never say anything so stupid again for the rest of my entire life."

Juliet hugged him. "I'm glad to hear you're getting smarter with age." She walked toward the door, but then turned and took a few steps back toward him. "Dylan, Fiona wasn't the one for you. Her life was cut short and that's so sad, and a baby was killed and that's tragic."

"Juliet—"

"Dylan, I don't want to see you lose Shelby."

Dylan walked over and put his hands on his sister's shoulders. He could remember not so long ago when she would've flinched if he had done that and was pleased to see she didn't now.

"Jules, if you're going to say that I've used Fiona's death as an excuse to keep everyone at arm's length, you're right. And that it's not only her death that's haunted me, but the fact that I knew I had gotten married to the wrong woman. And that's why I haven't let myself get close to anyone. I've already figured that out."

Juliet laughed and reached up to kiss Dylan on the cheek. "Actually, I was just going to say don't screw this up with Shelby."

She winked and left, leaving Dylan alone in the waiting room.

Yeah, Dylan had been afraid of letting Shelby get too close. But seeing her bleeding out right in front of him, watching her slip away from him in a way he couldn't stop?

That was when Dylan had learned true fear.

A nurse came out. "Ms. Keelan is awake. Would you like to see your fiancée?"

Dylan hoped Shelby wouldn't be upset by that little piece of news. It was the best way for him to be allowed to see her, since he wasn't her relative. And the fact that he had his entire family there backing him up had helped.

Shelby's mother was on her way. She should be here soon. Dylan wasn't very sure how she would take the fiancée news either. But he'd burn that bridge when he got to it.

Dylan followed the nurse into the intensive care unit. "You can only stay for ten minutes. But I'll be surprised if she's awake that long."

Shelby looked so tiny and frail in the bed. Little, and not at all fierce. He slid a lock of her hair back away from her face and her eyes opened. They still seemed a little unfocused, but at least they weren't clouded with pain this time.

"Megan and the baby are okay?" Shelby whispered.

"Yes, they weren't hurt at all."

"And we stopped the bomb at the memorial?"

"Yep, nobody hurt there, either." Dylan ran a finger down her cheek. "Nobody got hurt at all, but you, Freckles."

"And Chantelle DiMuzio is a—"

Dylan half coughed and half laughed as a filthy set of words about Chantelle DiMuzio flew out of

Shelby's mouth. Even a nurse looked over, eyebrow raised, from the station in the center of the room.

But seeing the state Shelby was in, knowing how much she had fought just to be alive now? Dylan didn't mind Shelby saying that and could add a few choice words of his own, although he didn't.

"Um, yes. Chantelle was not a nice person. And was the traitor. And is no longer among the living, so we probably don't need to call her any more names."

"But I want to. I don't like her." Shelby's voice was beginning to slur. Dylan could tell she was fading.

"Sleep now. You can say as many terrible things as you want when you wake up," he promised.

THREE DAYS LATER Shelby was beginning to wish she had died in that alley. Okay, maybe not really, but a little bit.

This hospital was her description of hell.

There were people around her all the time. She was never alone, someone was always talking to her, asking questions. And Shelby had to answer them politely. Because they were her caregivers and were only doing their job. And what kind of terrible person would Shelby be if she was mean to the people who had taken such good care of her?

She wondered if she could sneak out. Maybe go out the window.

Probably not, since she couldn't even walk five feet to the bathroom without assistance.

And to make all of these matters worse, Shelby's mother, Belinda, was here. She'd already asked Shelby, oh, so subtly, if Shelby would like her to put on a little makeup—*you know, sweetie, to cover up some of those freckles*—and do Shelby's hair. It was important to look good, even in the hospital—*you know, sweetie, because there's just so many attractive nurses around*—for one's fiancé.

Fiancé.

Dylan had explained that it had been the easiest way for him to have access to her when she'd first been brought into the hospital. Shelby didn't blame him, as a matter of fact, thought it was kind of sweet.

But then a nurse had told her mother about Shelby's *fiancé*. And that had been it. After meeting Dylan, her mother had actually cried tears of joy. Belinda had thought Shelby would never find someone who would put up with her and all her awkwardness.

That was a direct quote. That Belinda had said to pretty much everyone.

Shelby had tried to explain. Even Dylan had tried to explain. But every time they did, Belinda just started crying and thanking heaven her little girl was alive and had found someone to love. And then promptly changed the subject.

Shelby closed her eyes and shook her head. She knew when she opened them, the huge stack of bridal and wedding magazines her mom had brought in and set by her bed would be the first thing she saw.

So, yeah, a little bit Shelby wished she had just moved on to a better place in that alley.

The sole peace she got was when she worked with Megan to decipher more of the DS-13 code. Now that all the data from Shelby's head was in the Omega system, Megan could bring it in to the hospital in smaller chunks on a laptop. Although Shelby was only able to work short spurts at a time before exhaustion set in, they'd cracked away at it multiple times each day.

They'd found four more potential bomb sites and dates as well as information about the key people responsible for each likely attack. Megan, as well as all the other Bransons who stopped by, assured Shelby that the information from the codes would put an end to DS-13 for good. Arrests were already being made.

So although the mental exertion tired Shelby, she was glad to help. Plus, Megan always shooed

Belinda out of Shelby's hospital room while they worked, making deciphering the code Shelby's favorite activity ever.

They were releasing her from the hospital tomorrow, but Shelby would need someone to help her around the clock for at least the next week. She was glad to be going, to be getting away from all these people, most especially her mother, before she went absolutely crazy.

Her mom came bouncing through the door, no doubt having just been flirting with some doctor significantly younger than her. Shelby knew she couldn't wait any longer. She needed to tell her mother her plans for once Shelby was released from the hospital.

"Mother, I've decided to go home tomorrow after they release me."

"Home where, darling? With Dylan?"

"No. To my home. To my condo in Knoxville. I'm just going to hire a temporary nurse to take care of me."

Belinda immediately went over and began pressing the nurse call button next to Shelby's bed.

"Mother, what are you doing? That button is supposed to be for emergencies."

"It is an emergency. Listen to the crazy way you are talking!" Belinda's volume never rose, but her intensity did.

And, of course, Dylan picked that moment to walk in.

"Evening, ladies. Everything okay?"

"Oh, thank goodness you're here, Dylan. Something is wrong with Shelby."

Dylan looked over at Shelby with concern, but Shelby just rolled her eyes.

"There's nothing wrong with me, Mother."

Just then, the nurse walked in, so Shelby repeated her assertion that she was fine and apologized for accidentally hitting the call button.

"Dylan, Shelby plans to go all the way back to Knoxville and have some stranger care for her. You simply cannot allow her to do that. Tell her."

"The doctors estimate I'll need care for one week, Mother. I am pretty wealthy. Hiring someone for a week shouldn't be a problem," she told them both. "I've already got my assistant looking into it."

Dylan leaned over and whispered something in Belinda's ear. Belinda nodded and patted his hand, then walked out of the room.

"I don't even want to know what you just said to her."

Dylan chuckled. "Yeah, you really don't."

Dylan came over and sat on her bed. "I know this fiancé thing has gotten a little bit out of control with your mom, and I'm so sorry."

"Yeah, my mother is one of a kind." Shelby rolled her eyes.

"I want to ask you for one thing. Let me handle the details of your next week's care. I think I can safely say that I've learned a few things about your needs and your quirks, as you call them."

"Dylan—"

"Shelby, give us a chance to get to know each other with no plane crashes, or snakes, or bombs, or guns. If after a week we're ready to get rid of each other, then that's okay. But let me do this for you."

Shelby didn't want him to feel as if he was responsible for her. "Are you sure you want to?"

"I've never been more sure of anything."

Shelby hesitated, torn. Was she just prolonging the inevitable? If Dylan was still in love with his wife, what would a week change?

"Please, Freckles."

Shelby nodded. "Just promise, whoever's house we're staying at, tell them not to give their address to my mother."

Chapter Twenty-Six

Borrowing a plane from Omega hadn't been a problem for Dylan. After all Shelby and Dylan had done, and because now Dennis Burgamy was their friend rather than adversary, Dylan had been given access to whatever he needed.

"Whose house are we going to?" Shelby had asked as they left the hospital. "Back to Cameron and Sophia's?"

Dylan didn't want to share Shelby with anyone. He was taking her back to his house in Falls Run.

He'd already been home yesterday, before Shelby had even agreed to let Dylan take care of her. There were some changes he'd had to make around his house before she got there. Some were medically necessary to help her out over the next week.

Some he hoped would be enough to help erase the hurt he'd caused her with his careless words at the table a few mornings ago. And some he hoped would convince her to stay longer than a week.

She'd been surprised when after leaving the hospital they'd pulled up at a small airstrip outside town rather than at the house of one of his siblings. "Where are we going?"

"Back to Falls Run. To my house."

Because of her injury and surgery, Shelby couldn't fly in the cockpit with Dylan. He helped her get situated in the cabin, lying across two reclining seats. He kissed her on the forehead and told her to get some rest. Soon they were in the air.

It was probably good that they couldn't talk during the flight. Both of them had heavy things on their minds.

Shelby made her concerns known immediately after they landed, before she would even get out of the plane.

"I didn't know we were going to your house when I agreed to do this," she told him.

"I know." That's why he hadn't told her. He was afraid she'd say no.

"You're still in love with your wife." Shelby believed in getting to the point. It was one of the things Dylan enjoyed most about her.

But about this, she was wrong.

"No. Shelby, I grieve for the loss of her young life, and definitely the baby's, but I wasn't even in love with her when she died. I realized that's the biggest part of what kept me trapped with her ghost for so long. Not so much the fear of losing, but the fear of *choosing* wrong like I had with her."

Shelby seemed to ponder that.

"Are we still okay? Will you still give me the week?"

Shelby nodded and Dylan scooped her up in his arms and carried her off the plane and down to his truck. He went back and got the little luggage they had, then closed the hangar door behind him. He drove slowly over the rough road leading to his house and parked as close to the front steps as possible.

He got out and walked around to her side of the truck and opened the door. This was it.

Dylan had never felt more unsure of himself in his entire life. It wasn't a feeling he was used to or enjoyed.

He trailed a finger down Shelby's cheek and helped her out of the truck. "I know that Sawyer and Megan's good-mornings that meant so much to them touched you. Sawyer has always been great with romantic stuff like that. But I'm not, Shelby. I'm sorry."

Dylan felt completely inadequate. What he'd done wasn't romantic. She was just going to think he was nuts. He helped her walk up the porch stairs slowly.

"I know you only promised me a week, Shelby, but I hope you'll give me—give us—much longer. And you trusted me to make you as comfortable as possible—" Dylan opened his front door "—so I hope you don't mind that I did this."

He helped Shelby through the front door and into the living room. Where he had moved her favorite overstuffed chair from her condo, the time-out chair she had told him about, that helped her know everything would be all right. He'd put it in between the front window and the fireplace, thinking she could enjoy the view and be warm.

"How?" she whispered.

"I contacted your assistant and she let me into your apartment yesterday. After thoroughly vetting that I was who I said I was and that I wasn't just robbing you, of course."

Shelby was just standing there, saying nothing, staring at the chair.

Dylan laughed and it sounded awkward even to his own ears. "I was trying to be romantic, but I'm obviously not as good at it as Sawyer."

Dylan walked over to the MP3 player on the end table by her chair. He turned it on. "And I recorded about six hours' worth of traffic from right outside your window. I know how you love that traffic sound."

Shelby still hadn't said anything. Dylan turned off the MP3 and looked at her. She had both hands covering her face and was crying.

"Shelby, are you okay? Are you hurting?" Dylan rushed to her side.

Shelby immediately put both hands on his cheeks. "This is the most special and romantic thing anyone has ever done for me. It's good-mornings enough to last a lifetime."

"Then promise me you'll stay a lifetime here with me and know that every time you turn on the sound of that traffic that I love you."

"You can bet on it because I love you, too."

He tenderly picked her up in his arms and sat them both in her time-out chair. He'd take time-out with her there every chance he got. The two of them together were a perfect fit.

* * * * *

LARGER-PRINT BOOKS!

◆ HARLEQUIN

Presents®

GET 2 FREE LARGER-PRINT NOVELS PLUS 2 FREE GIFTS!

PASSION
GUARANTEED
SEDUCTION

YES! Please send me 2 FREE LARGER-PRINT Harlequin Presents® novels and my 2 FREE gifts (gifts are worth about $10). After receiving them, if I don't wish to receive any more books, I can return the shipping statement marked "cancel." If I don't cancel, I will receive 6 brand-new novels every month and be billed just $5.30 per book in the U.S. or $5.74 per book in Canada. That's a saving of at least 12% off the cover price! It's quite a bargain! Shipping and handling is just 50¢ per book in the U.S. and 75¢ per book in Canada.* I understand that accepting the 2 free books and gifts places me under no obligation to buy anything. I can always return a shipment and cancel at any time. Even if I never buy another book, the two free books and gifts are mine to keep forever.

176/376 HDN GHVY

Name	(PLEASE PRINT)

Address	Apt. #

City	State/Prov.	Zip/Postal Code

Signature (if under 18, a parent or guardian must sign)

Mail to the **Reader Service:**
IN U.S.A.: P.O. Box 1867, Buffalo, NY 14240-1867
IN CANADA: P.O. Box 609, Fort Erie, Ontario L2A 5X3

**Are you a subscriber to Harlequin Presents® books and want to receive the larger-print edition?
Call 1-800-873-8635 today or visit us at www.ReaderService.com.**

* Terms and prices subject to change without notice. Prices do not include applicable taxes. Sales tax applicable in N.Y. Canadian residents will be charged applicable taxes. Offer not valid in Quebec. This offer is limited to one order per household. Not valid for current subscribers to Harlequin Presents Larger-Print books. All orders subject to credit approval. Credit or debit balances in a customer's account(s) may be offset by any other outstanding balance owed by or to the customer. Please allow 4 to 6 weeks for delivery. Offer available while quantities last.

Your Privacy—The Reader Service is committed to protecting your privacy. Our Privacy Policy is available online at www.ReaderService.com or upon request from the Reader Service.

We make a portion of our mailing list available to reputable third parties that offer products we believe may interest you. If you prefer that we not exchange your name with third parties, or if you wish to clarify or modify your communication preferences, please visit us at www.ReaderService.com/consumerschoice or write to us at Reader Service Preference Service, P.O. Box 9062, Buffalo, NY 14240-9062. Include your complete name and address.

HPLP15

LARGER-PRINT BOOKS!
GET 2 FREE LARGER-PRINT NOVELS PLUS
2 FREE GIFTS!

H HARLEQUIN®

super romance®

More Story...More Romance